STANDING HEAVY

GauZ'

STANDING HEAVY

Translated from the French by
Frank Wynne

BIBLIOASIS
Windsor, Ontario

First published in the French language as
Debout-payé by Le Nouvel Attila, 2014

First published in North America
by Biblioasis, 2023

FIRST EDITION

1 3 5 7 9 10 8 6 4 2

Library and Archives Canada Cataloguing in Publication

Title: Standing heavy / Gauz' ; translated
from the French by Frank Wynne.
Other titles: Debout-payé. English
Names: Gauz, 1971- author. | Wynne, Frank, translator.
Series: Biblioasis international translation series ; 43.
Description: Series statement: Biblioasis international
translation series | Translation of: Debout-payé.
Identifiers: Canadiana (print) 2023047800X | Canadiana
(ebook) 20230478034 | ISBN 9781771966009
(softcover) | ISBN 9781771966016 (EPUB)
Classification: LCC PQ3989.3.G38 D4313 2023 | DDC 843/.92—dc23

Published through the intermediary of the literary
agency BooksAgent – France (www.booksagent.fr)

This book is supported by the
Institut français (Royaume-Uni)
as part of the Burgess programme.

Readied for the press by Daniel Wells
Designed and typeset in Nocturne by Patty Rennie
Cover designed by Nathan Burton

PRINTED AND BOUND IN CANADA

For Céline

Sephora . . . my niece, my dove
This country's perfect scent
Your papá, Armand, sent
These laughing words above.

PROLOGUE

NEW RECRUITS

The Black men mounting the narrow staircase look like climbers roped together for an assault on K2, the most fearsome peak in the Himalayas. Their ascent is punctuated only by the sound of feet on stairs, footsteps muffled by a thick red carpet laid precisely in the middle of a stairwell so narrow that two men cannot pass. The steps are steep, and knees are raised high. Nine treads, a landing, then nine more, make a floor. With each floor, the weary mountaineers become more spaced out. From time to time, there comes the sound of someone catching his breath. Reaching the sixth floor, the first in line presses the button of the cyclopean intercom, its lone eye the black lens of a security camera. The vast office in which they find themselves, bathed in sweat, is open-plan. No walls interrupt the space between the men, and the glass cage is emblazoned with the three letters that mark the territory of the dominant male of this place: CEO. A huge picture window generously affords a view over the rooftops of Paris. Forms are handed out. Left, right and centre. Here, they are recruiting. They are recruiting security guards. Project-75 has just been granted several major security contracts for a variety of commercial properties in the Paris area. They are in urgent need of massive manpower. Word quickly spread through the African "community". Congolese, Ivoirians, Malians, Guineans, Beninese, Senegalese, etc., the keen eye can easily identify each country by its style of clothing. The polo shirt and Levi 501 combo of the Ivoirians; the baggy leather jackets of the Malians; the striped shirts tucked below the paunches of the Beninese and the Togolese; the beautiful, perfectly polished moccasins of the Cameroonians; the preposterous colours of the Congolese from Brazzaville and the outrageous style of the Congolese from Kinshasa ... If there is any doubt, the ear takes over because, in the mouths of Africans, the intonations of the French language are markers that designate origin as reliably as a third copy of chromosome 21 indicates Down's syndrome or a malignant tumour denotes cancer. The Congolese modulate, the Cameroonians sing-song, the Senegalese chant, the Ivoirians falter, the Beninese and the Togolese waver, the Malians speak pidgin ...

Everyone takes out the various papers required for the interview: identity cards, the traditional CVs and CQPs, a kind of official permit to work in security. Here, it is portentously dubbed a *diploma*. There is the famous motivational letter: "To whom it may concern"; "part of a dynamic team"; "a profession with ambitious career prospects"; "in keeping with my skills and training"; "please be assured"; "in anticipation of a favourable response"; "Yours faithfully", etc. In such a place, the medieval circumlocutions and arse-licking phrases of covering letters seem risible. Everyone here has a powerful motivation, although it may be very different depending on which side of the glass one finds oneself. For the dominant male in the glass cage at the far end of the open-plan office, it is maximum turnover. By any means necessary. Hiring as many people as possible is part of the means. For the Black procession in the stairwell, it is an escape from unemployment or a zero-hours contract. By any means necessary. Security guarding is one of those means. It's relatively accessible. The training is absolutely minimal. No experience is required. Employers are all too willing to overlook official status. The morphological profile is supposedly appropriate. Morphological profile ... Black men are heavy-set; Black men are tall; Black men are strong; Black men are deferential; Black men are scary. It is impossible not to think of this jumble of "noble savage" clichés lurking atavistically in the minds of every White man responsible for recruitment and every Black man who has come to use these clichés to his advantage. But that is not the issue this morning. No-one cares. And besides, there are Black men on the recruiting team. The atmosphere is relaxed. Someone even ventures a couple of lewd remarks about the prominent breasts of one of the two secretaries charged with handing out the recruitment forms. Everyone fills out his form with a modicum of diligence. Surname, first name, sex, date and place of birth, marital status, social security number, etc. This will be the most demanding intellectual challenge of the morning. Even so, a few of the men glance at their neighbour's form. A legacy of the classroom, or a lack of self-assurance. Someone coming out of a long period of unemployment lacks self-assurance. Papers in every possible combination are passed between the group of Negroes and the secretary with the big tits. After signing and initialling a few white pages blackened with esoteric phrases intended to regulate the working relationship with the soon-to-be-ex-unemployed and the soon-to-be-big-boss, every member of the group is given a bag containing a pair of black trousers, a black jacket, a black tie, a shirt that may be white or black and a monthly work rota indicating the time and place of shifts. The contracts are open-ended. Every man who came into these offices unemployed leaves as a security guard. Those who already have experience in the profession know what lies in store in the coming days: spending all day standing in a shop, repeating this monotonous exercise in tedium every day, until the end of the month comes, and they are paid. Paid standing. And it is not as easy as it might seem. In order to survive in this job, to keep things in perspective, to avoid lapsing into cosy idleness or, on the contrary, fatuous zeal and bitter aggressiveness, requires either knowing how to empty your mind of every thought higher than instinct and spinal reflex or having a very engrossing inner life. The incorrigible idiot option is also highly prized. Each to his own method. Each to his own goals. Each will walk back down the six floors in his own way.

THE CHAPEL AT "LA CHAPELLE"

Bar run by a Kabyle from Algeria, Chinese clothes shop run by a man from Nanjing, Tunisian bakery, little Pakistani hardware shop, Indian jewellers, another bar run by another Kabyle but frequented by Senegalese, Tamil mini-cab company, another Pakistani hardware shop, Algerian butcher, another Chinese clothes shop – this one run by a man from Wenzhou – second-hand clothes shop run by a Moroccan, Wenzhou-Chinese bar-tabac, Turkish restaurant – not to be confused with the Kurdish kebab shop next door – another Algerian butcher – this one from Djurdjura – Balkan boutique, Moroccan grocer specialising in African and West Indian food, another-other Kabyle bar, mini-mall of second-hand goods run by a sullen Slav, Korean electronics shop, branch of Topy shoe repairs run by a guy from Mali, Tamil hardware shop, another Moroccan grocer, another-other Kabyle bar frequented by preterminal alcoholics, African grocers run by a Korean, clandestine Croatian casino, Tamil hairdresser, Algerian hairdresser, African hairdresser from Côte d'Ivoire, Cameroonian grocer, West Indian shop selling arcane objects and *bwa bandé*, Jewish medical laboratory... walking down the rue du Faubourg du Temple is like taking a stroll along the tower of Babel if it had been expertly toppled by a demolition crew such that, rather than standing vertical, it runs horizontally from Belleville to place de la République. What if *this* is the hidden treasure of the Knights Templar, this incredible diversity of civilisations and cultures that line the streets where their Great Temple once stood? At Goncourt métro, the avenue Parmentier traces a perpendicular. Here the atmosphere is more Parisian, more French, more globalised Western, more "normal": hipster bar; branch of Caisse d'Épargne; traditional French boulangerie with rustic, floury French baguettes; branch of Crédit Lyonnais; Italian pizzeria; branch of Crédit Agricole; Apple authorised dealer; bookseller and stationer; branch of BNP Paribas; restaurant mentioned in Michelin and Hachette guides; branch of Crédit Mutuel; company specialising in acoustics; branch of Société Générale; secondary school named after some dead French guy; branch of HSBC; shoe shop specialising in plus sizes; another branch of Crédit Lyonnais; two primary schools with plaques listing the names of children deported to the camps during the Second World War; municipal swimming pool ... Heading east, you come to the town hall of the eleventh arrondissement, with its gilding and the Tricolour fluttering above a grey slate roof, a quintessential building of the French Republic. From here, visiting the branch of Camaïeu, a women's clothing outlet, on the rue du Faubourg-Saint-Antoine feels to Ossiri like time travel.

Back in the days of "La Chapelle", Ossiri and Kassoum paced the streets of the area systematically, like surveyors.

Situated in the shadow of the angel's gilded arse atop the pillar on the place de la Bastille, this part of the eleventh arrondissement, along with the Champs-Élysées, was one of the great night spots of Paris. The cool bars, the concept bars, the exotic restaurants from every latitude, the lounge bars, private clubs, nightclubs, dance bars and small concert venues all drew huge crowds every night, especially on weekends. In its less entertaining mode, this neighbourhood also boasted the highest number of Chinese clothes factories. In poorly ventilated, windowless rooms, in dark yards, converted patios, modified atriums and refurbished halls, armies of Chinese workers, most of them illegals, worked night and day to pay off their debts to people smugglers. Aside from the noisy Chinese New Year, they had no rest, no holidays. The Chinese employers earned on the backs of such model employees – top model even. The production costs for fashionable dresses were very low in a country where both living standards and consumerism were very high. To have an army of skilled, underpaid, non-unionised, easily exploited workers in the heart of Paris was called onshore offshoring. A considerable capitalist coup for the Chinese. As a result, the binge-drinkers partying in the Bastille area were among the privileged few in France who could throw up their skinful of booze in front of the doors used by the workers who made the very clothes, now rank with stale smoke, in which they had just spent the night pulsating, sweating and dancing.

The spectacle of late-night party animals who were somewhat the worse for wear, especially on Sundays, was one of the things that Kassoum and Ossiri most enjoyed sharing. To make way for Zandro, the resident physiognomist at La Chapelle des Lombards, one of the most popular nightclubs in Bastille, they had to get up at the crack of dawn and leave the tiny studio they naturally dubbed the "Chapel", since it was right above the nightclub. Since they did not have work every day and did not always know where to go so early in the morning, they would spend the early hours with the last of the revellers. Ossiri and Kassoum were fresh and wide-eyed. The straggling party animals were tired, drunk and wasted. With the old reflexes of a child of the Treichville slums,[1] Kassoum could not help but think of these prancing peacocks as easy prey, ready to be relieved of a little jewellery or money; he had had considerable experience back in Abidjan. But Ossiri seemed to be able to read his every thought and, with a look, could rein him in. "Leave the vultures' work to the vultures," he would often say. And Kassoum would content himself with finding a prime viewing post to look and laugh at the late-night, early hours circus of Parisians and suburbanites. Even the night when a girl who was three sheets to the wind threw herself at him, shrieking *"Take me! Take me!"* in English, Ossiri did not succumb. Her gaping handbag revealed a wad of blue €20 notes that seemed to plead with Kassoum for the safe asylum of his pockets. He hadn't seen so much as a euro in more than a week, and here was

---

1 Author's note: A poor district of Abidjan.

a yawning handbag that Fologo, the most ham-fisted pick-pocket in all the shantytowns from Colosse to Treichville, could have lifted without attracting attention.

"Kass, leave the vultures' work to the vultures."

"Take me! Take me!"

"Come on! She's practically giving it away. When a player on the other team scores an own goal, there's no off-side, Ossiri."

"Take me! Take me!"

"What's she saying?"

"She really wants me to take her. I swear, she's taunting me."

"Lay one finger on her, and you don't know me anymore."

"Take me! Take me!"

"Fucking rich boy's son!"

"Fucking rich boy's son!" was the phrase that signalled Kassoum's capitulation whenever the two of them disagreed on how best to earn a crust when times were hard. When the girl started throwing up over his jacket and then over his shoes, Kassoum decided to "awaken the ghetto" in himself and deliver a lunging python – a quick, well-placed, keenly felt head-butt, "a lethal head-butt" of the kind that had made his reputation and ensured that everyone in the sprawling ghetto of Colosse was wary of hand-to-hand combat with him. "Ossiri, I spent years and years sleeping in the ghetto. Now, it's like the ghetto is sleeping in me."

But something in the girl's eyes made him pause, and the python refused to lunge. Kassoum could not quite tell what it was. Distress, maybe. The sort of distress he had often seen in the eyes of his neighbours in Colosse who did not know how to begin another day that, even before it began, was destined to be as wretched as the day before. Or was it the pale green of the girl's irises? Who on earth has green eyes? In the folktales of his childhood, certain monsters were described as having green eyes, eyes the colour of the forest's depths. Kassoum had never been so close to eyes this colour. His unease must have been palpable.

Behind him, Ossiri pressed his advantage, suggesting that they take the girl back to the Chapel and look after her until she came to her senses. Zandro would not say anything; he would probably not even notice. He was always too wound up by a night spent dealing with the thugs, the hysterics, the pickpockets, the drunkards, the queue-jumpers, the drama queens, the paranoiacs, the depressives, the drug dealers, the junkies and all the hotheads who thought they were the strongest men in the world after a line of coke or a couple of bombs of MDMA. Kassoum carried the girl up the narrow stairwell on his own. Her long blonde hair fell over her judoka's shoulders, and, even in her inebriated state, she looked fearsome. This girl was clearly a descendant of the White tribe from the glacial Great North. Those who routinely pillaged the more southerly shores of Europe, spreading terror, chaos and spermatozoa. Ossiri made no move to help her, on the grounds that, even in Bastille, the sight of two Black men leading a half-comatose White girl down a dark, deserted street would seem suspect. In this, he was not wrong, but as so often, he pushed his reasoning much too far. "Since the Second World War, ratting people out has gone from being a sport in France to a national institution. When the Germans occupied the country, people turned in Jews and resistance fighters. When the Allies won the war, those same people turned in traitors and collaborators. In France, there are always sell-outs and people to be sold," Ossiri said imperiously. But Kassoum had already stopped listening. Like a panther with a deer in its maw scaling a tree to hide its prey from a pack of covetous, carrion-eating hyenas, he lugged the strapping wench towards the Chapel. This is how Kassoum came to meet Amélie, who came from Normandy and taught secondary school English in a suburb in west Paris . . .

The town hall of the eleventh arrondissement overlooks a roundabout that alternately sends vehicles ricocheting along the avenue Parmentier, the boulevard Voltaire, the rue de la Roquette and the avenue Ledru-Rollin. At the junction with the rue du Faubourg-Saint-Antoine stands a branch of Monoprix. Tantie Odette has been the manager here for two years. She was previously a checkout girl for twenty-eight years. Thirty years ago, when her husband had her sent from a village nestled by the great forests to the west of Côte d'Ivoire, she could scarcely read or write and had never before seen humans of any race other than that which, for thousands of years, had loped beneath the liana-shrouded trees in Issia. "Auntie" has seen and learned many things working in this branch of Monoprix. Even so, it took twenty-eight years before she was allowed to emerge from behind the checkout counter ... Was this fast-track promotion at the speed of melanin? She has long since stopped asking herself such questions. She is two years from retirement. Since Ossiri started working security at the Bastille branch of Camaïeu two weeks ago, his visits to this branch of Monoprix have almost taken on the form of a ritual. Tantie Odette offers him coffee. He accepts. They go into the break room. He asks for news of Ferdinand. In gruff monosyllables, she tells him what she has heard. She asks for news of Angela. He makes up stories, weaves lyrical phrases through the more general rumours from the old country. She laughs. She laughs a lot when he talks to her. Then he takes his leave, protesting that he will be late. She walks him back through the aisles, never missing the opportunity to introduce him as her son when some former colleague from the 1980s happens by. A kiss on the cheek as Ossiri unchains his bicycle from the sign that reads "NO BICYCLES". Camaïeu is nearby. He walks.

THE SALES
AT CAMAÏEU

THE REGULARS

These women buy clothes as though they were perishable goods. They pop in every month, every week, every day, sometimes several times a day. Regular customers are easily recognisable. They are always the ones in a tearing hurry. They know what they want. They never stay long.

PSYCHEDELIA

A field of vision limited to the blinding glare from the spotlights set into in the false ceiling and the gaudy orange signs emblazoned with the famous "%" sign that screams "SALE!" Lying on her back in a stroller, a baby has her first psychedelic experience while her mother shops the sales.

HANDBAG

In a women's clothes shop, any woman with a bag has no need to linger by the tiny little display of hideous handbags...unless she is attempting a little shoplifting. She stuffs the booty into her own bag. Into the handbag on the rail, she stuffs the anti-theft tags she carefully snipped off with a pair of pliers while she was in the changing room. An unequal exchange of merchandise.

THE LAW OF THE HANDBAG

In a women's clothing shop, all the women are permanently attached to their handbags, especially the thieves.

THE CAMAÏEU DICTUM

In a clothes shop, a customer without a bag is a customer who will not steal.

RADIO CAMAÏEU

This is the music played in the shop throughout the day. In every ten songs played on Radio Camaïeu, seven feature female singers, two are duets with men, only one features a solo by a man. Assuming each song lasts three minutes, meaning twenty songs an hour, a security guard can expect to be exposed to 120 musical horrors in the space of a six-hour shift. Truly, the shift break is one of the greatest achievements negotiated by trade unions.

RIGHT BUTTOCKS

Although it is possible to distinguish a number of broad groups, the shape of a person's buttocks is as unique as their fingerprint. Then the security guard begins to wonder what would happen in police stations if this were the system of identification adopted by the authorities.

LEFT BUTTOCKS

African women rarely buy anything other than tops because of their callipygian anatomy. Trousers, shorts, culottes and the like are made according to the vital statistics of the average White woman, who is naturally flat, by women in Chinese factories, who are naturally flat.

In China, apparently the word "buttock" does not exist. There, they simply say "lower back". It is impossible to invent a word for a part of the body that does not exist.

CHINESE WOMAN

Given the percentage of the Camaïeu clothes that come from the country of Mao, you could argue that a Chinese woman shopping here is reclaiming her heritage.

DIALOGUE

Man: Why are you following me around?

Woman: Yeah, why are you following us around? This is harassment!

Security Guard: I'm sorry, I wasn't following you around. Well, not you in particular.

Man: That's a lie! Take a look in the pushchair: there's nothing in there. Why don't you go harass those French people over there instead of stalking us?

Security Guard: You're paranoid, monsieur.

Man: What?

Security Guard: You're *pa-ra-noid*.

Man: No, I'm not! I'm *Al-ge-ri-an*.

ANTI-THEFT TAGS
AND CHANGING ROOMS

Barefoot women dressed in clothes they are considering buying regularly walk out of the changing room in search of something in a different size or colour. The clothes they are trying on are decked with price tags and grey, plastic anti-theft devices shaped like flying saucers attached to the fabric.

- *Sleeveless dresses*: the garment tag hangs from the armpit. The anti-theft device is pinned to the right buttock. The price tag is on the back.
- *Trousers*: there is a tag on the right hip. There is another on the left thigh next to the markdown sticker (50% off!); this one is a long, translucent plastic strip stuck to the fabric. The price tag is on the left hip; sometimes a "Wash Care" label is attached to the back of the waistband and dangles over the cleft of the buttocks.
- *Blouses and shirts*: the markdown is on a strip stuck to the left shoulder; there is a plastic strip on the left sleeve, while the price tag protrudes from the middle of the belly.

For a woman trying on a pair of *Carlita* jeans and a *Tolérant* top, this amounts to:

- €24.95, with a markdown of 50%, for the legs and the buttocks.
- €14.95, with a markdown of 30%, for the breasts and the torso.

In other words, a total sale price of €22.94 to completely envelop all secondary sexual characteristics.

FAT WOMEN

Often, fat women will start by picking out clothes in smaller sizes ... before discreetly disappearing into a changing cubicle with the correct size.

THE BACK ROOM

In the stockroom, there are the toilets, the metal lockers assigned to staff, a fridge, a microwave and, most importantly, a bulletin board on which is written: "Tough Week negative T/O + Sales Coefficient + 9.91% = PRIME ☺ Keep at it!" (Punctuation and emoji obligatory.)

THE CUTE LITTLE TOP

"*OMG, this little top is just sooooo cute!*" This is one of the most common phrases used to describe the tops sold at Camaïeu. It is always said with head bowed, eyelashes fluttering, chin holding the aforementioned "cute little top" as it is carefully held taut against the breasts. The presence of an appreciative female friend is optional.

THE FASHION-CONSCIOUS TROPIQUETTES

The fashionista gaggles of young Black girls who spend endless hours in changing rooms talking clothes while trying on clothes. A bit like those French people who talk about food over dinner. The blood is in the culture, not on the skin, dammit.

TONSORIAL METAMORPHOSES

Fatima, the manager, has lost the beautiful black curly locks of the Maghreb she was sporting last week. Now her hair is as straight and blonde as a Viking queen's.

No-one has ever seen the glorious frizzy mane of Christiane, the Black sales assistant. She wears a long, synthetic-hair weave that tumbles down her back.

CRUDE OIL AND ALPHA-KERATIN

In his two weeks working as a security guard, no Black woman has come into the shop with natural hair. They all have wigs, weaves and hair extensions made from synthetic fibres derived from the oil industry. Crude oil, the primary source of global energy, is the result of the anaerobic decay of all prehistoric organic matter that has accumulated deep beneath the Earth's crust. Black women wear fossil fuels on their heads.

The security guard spots a Black woman with a long, flowing mane of hair that falls to her waist. Such a hairstyle required at least a tribe of Tyrannosaurs to rot and decay.

THE THEORY OF HAIR ENVY

Hair envy, as a phenomenon, tends northward: the Beurette, whose parents hailed from North Africa, longs for the straight, blonde mane of the Viking; the Tropiquette, whose parents came from countries in sub-Saharan Africa, longs for the curly locks of the Beurette.

BWWB

Bété Woman with White Baby. At a glance, the security guard recognises the "Bété Woman with White Baby". These are women of the Bété people from the Gagnoa region of Côte d'Ivoire. Most of those living in France are "childminders".

CHILDMINDER

An appropriately quasi-military term used to designate nannies employed to care for Western children who are half-princeling, half-prisoner.

TRADITIONAL BWWB

The security guard is transfixed by the fantastical image of a BWWB entering the shop bare-breasted, with a traditional skirt of woven raffia leaves tied around her waist. Reality, however, is quickly restored. In fact, she is pushing a two-seater buggy carrying two sleeping blonde cherubs. The BWWB is wearing a "cute little top" in polyamide fabric and a scruffy pair of jeans.

BWWB DIALOGUE

BWWB 1, staring contemptuously at a pair of stonewashed jeans: "I don't buy no wôrô-wôrô[2] jeans, they fall apart too quick."

BWWB 2, nodding vehemently: "You are right, sister. What are they thinking to put holes in jeans before we even buy them? Tchrrrr!"[3]

---

2 Author's note: wôrô-wôrô – the communal taxis in Abidjan, which are ramshackle and always breaking down.
3 Author's note: A distinctive whistle Africans make between lips and clenched teeth intended to signify disgust.

VOCABULARY

In the Ivoirian community in France, security is a profession so deeply rooted that it has spawned a specific terminology, one inflected with the colourful expressions from Nouchi, the popular slang of Abidjan.

Standing Heavy: designates all the various professions that require the employee to remain standing in order to earn a pittance.

Zagoli: specifically refers to the security guard. Zagoli Golié was a famous goalkeeper with Les Eléphants, the national team of Côte d'Ivoire. Being a security guard is like being a goalie: you stand there watching everyone else play, and, once in a while, you dive to catch the ball.

Soufè-wourou: literally "night-dog" in Malinke. The term refers to the "dog handlers", or "K-9 Specialist Security Agents" to use the official terminology. Although the position is significantly better paid, there are far fewer "soufè-wourou" than "zagoli" in the African community.

Traditionally, among the people of Sahelian and sub-Saharan Africa, excepting the Dozo, a caste of hunters dressed as scarecrows, Canids feature only in expressions like "mangy dog", "mongrel bastard" and "rabid dog" . . . As to their place in human society, there is little room for nuance.

The concept of the dog as man's best friend is a *Westernism* that is all too recent. So much so that the idea of choosing to have a dog as a companion and a work partner presents a cultural and psychological hurdle that is almost impossible to overcome for those who have grown up despising or fearing the raw-boned dogs – most suffering from mange or rabies – that roam the streets of African towns. Moreover, buying, feeding, training and providing for a dog represents a not insignificant initial financial investment when you are undocumented and unemployed. And if such an investment is required in order to secure a job, the process becomes like a dog chasing its tail. Ivoirians have decided "Zagoli is better!"

RADIO CAMAÏEU 2

I like your body
So, shake your booty
Let's get it on
And keep on pushing…

A significant number of female exponents of "neo soul", whether British, American or (the very worst) French, shriek mediocre lyrics over soupy melodies in a diluted version of the tortured, but genuinely extraordinary, Amy Winehouse.

How is it possible to allow such sub-singers to flourish and claim that what they sing is "soul", when Aretha Franklin is still with us? We no longer afford the illustrious dead the time or the common decency to turn in their graves. These days, we insult their memory while they're still alive.

FLOWER POWER

Laura and Rosa are two joyful sales assistants from the West Indies with floral names. From time to time, they improvise a few graceful dance moves to the songs played on Radio Camaïeu. Their hip-sway has the power to put a smile on the faces of every employee in the shop and the magical ability, for a few fleeting bars, to mitigate the talentless mediocrity of the screeching songstresses streaming from the speakers.

FIRST GENETIC THEORY OF THE ANTILLES

The colour of the skin, the colour of the eyes, the straightness of the hair, the shape of the nose, the lips, the buttocks... In the physiognomy of people from the Antilles, there is always at least one feature that serves as a reminder that the White master, the Béké, did not just wield a whip when it came to enslaved women. Perhaps one should say "females" out of respect for the language of the period.

SECOND GENETIC THEORY OF THE ANTILLES

When slavery existed, it was vanishingly rare, and almost impossible, for a Black male slave to procreate with a White mistress. It was therefore White masters who, with Black women, created the ethnic diversity of the Antillais. And, since it is the male who assigns the sex of the male child with his Y chromosome, we can therefore affirm that all mixed-race men in the Antilles definitely carry a Caucasian Y chromosome.

Abstract for the theory: in the Antilles, man is White, woman is Black.

BABIES

Initially a little intrigued, all babies eventually return the security guard's smile.

The security guard adores babies. Perhaps because babies do not shoplift.

Babies adore the security guard. Perhaps because he does not drag babies to the sales.

VERSION ANGLAISE

Given the throngs of foreign tourists, the branded bags in many boutiques translate "*SOLDES*" into English. Hence, the plastic bags from the Lacoste shop next door are emblazoned with the word "SALES". The security guard who works there says that some French families refuse to accept these bags. Apparently, they do not wish to lay themselves open to any linguistic confusion that might reflect poorly on their personal hygiene.

THE MOUSTACHIOED

A mother and daughter of striking similarity each sport downy moustaches that are highly visible. The girl, still in her teens, is sulky and exudes a profound world-weariness. The fifty-something mother, though a little severe, looks much more radiant. Having been blessed with this supra-labial hirsuteness, uncommon among women, for decades, probably since she was her daughter's age, she has had more than enough time to accept it or tolerate it. The daughter still has many years of sulking ahead of her.

The moustachioed mother and daughter come a second time. They are easily recognisable. The security guard offers a jaunty "hello" garnished with a beaming smile in the faint hope of cheering them up. The mother does not reply, nor does she even turn. The daughter looks daggers at him.

THE MOUSTACHE THEORY

Hitler, Stalin, Pinochet, the Bongos of Gabon, Saddam Hussein... For the dictator, the moustache is an external manifestation of inner contentment, whereas for a woman, especially in her teens, the moustache is a source of disquiet.

PROSPECTIVE HEIRESS

Having spent more than an hour wandering around the shop without actually buying anything, a woman turns to an elderly lady hunched over her walking frame: "Maman, let's go to the New Look across the road. They've got further reductions."

In the sweltering summer heat, the elderly lady, visibly drained, her mouth hanging open, does not complain but painfully follows her daughter.

THE LAPLACE TRANSFORM

How is it possible to be reminded of the Laplace transform when watching an old woman with a purple rinse rummaging through a dumpbin of *Gaby* – WAS €24.95: NOW 70% OFF! – goose-shit-green striped cardigans?

TATTOOS

The fine, delicate lines of the tattoo on her neck outline a lotus, one that is identical to the logo used by "Lotus" toilet paper. Against her pale skin, it looks as though she has a bog roll stuck between her head and her shoulders.

RETROVOLUTION

For centuries, piercings, scarification and tattoos have been considered the epitome of barbarous savagery in the Western popular imagination.

What, then, should we think of the countless pasty bodies covered with ink and riddled with piercings? The ethnic tattoos inscribed on pink flesh? Is it a fashion? Angst? A fashionable angst? An angsty fashion? The unconscious desire to return to the happy state of the noble savage?

REVOLUTION

These days, it is agreed that only seven haggard prisoners were languishing in the Bastille on July 14, 1789. In other words, there was hardly anyone to liberate. But history favours symbols over facts. Were it staged today, storming the Bastille, with its serried ranks of luxury shops, would liberate thousands of prisoners to conspicuous consumption.

THE LAPLACE TRANSFORM 2

The Laplace transform is a complex mathematical operation named after its inventor that makes it possible to describe the variation of certain functions (f) over time (t).

These days, it is used in *financial modelling*, i.e. to determine prices. For example, Laplace transforms are used to calculate the ideal markdowns and optimal prices during sales. A complex equation to regulate frivolous pleasures.

IPHONE

A young girl tries on a pair of glasses and studies her reflection on her iPhone, set to FaceTime. Next to her, there is a floor-to-ceiling mirror.

In fitting rooms, girls try on outfits and use their iPhones to photograph each other from every angle. They then gather around the screen to discuss their choices. The pixel has gained ascendency over the retina.

CHRISTLIKE

One arm extended towards the *Langouste* linen skirts, the other towards the *Laure* summer dresses, a woman genuflects before the *Victoire* miniskirts. Amen.

BLASPHEMY

On the clothes rail, almost a dozen of the sheath dresses are not "Made in China". They are "Made in Turkey". Practically in Europe!

THE ANGEL

The gilded angel still perches, naked, atop the column in the middle of the place de la Bastille. Given that seraphim are sexless, the angel could just as easily shop at Celio as at Camaïeu. But how to let it know that the sales are in full swing?

DIALOGUE

Woman, brandishing a price tag marked €29.99: 'Scuse me, how much is this with the 20% off, please?

Security guard: About six euros, Madame.

Woman: You know how it is, it's important to dress well, to move on with your life. I've just lost my husband.

Security guard: . . . !

Woman: Thank you, Monsieur. You're very kind. Now, where do I pay?

THE TEENAGER IN THE WHEELCHAIR

A disabled teenage girl glides past in an electric wheelchair. She is preceded by her sister and followed by her mother and her father. The back of the chair is fitted with a bar that can be used to manually push the chair. While in the shop, it serves to hang the outfits that she and her sister choose. Within an hour, it looks like a Camaïeu mobile display rail.

LOVERS

A pair of lovers are sloppily kissing next to the *Jakarta* display of garishly coloured dresses that look like curtains in a brothel. Meanwhile, on Radio Camaïeu, Brick & Lace are singing "Love is Wicked".

THE MODEL

Wearing a striped *Baléar* top and a pair of *Martinque* slacks, a woman steps into the shop already dressed head-to-toe in Camaïeu.

HADES

The *Hades* jacket is 100% pigskin leather. Is such a jacket off-limits to Muslims and Jews?

The Grand Mufti: "*Hades* – this jacket is Haram."

The Chief Rabbi: "*Hades* – this jacket is not Kosher."

The Great Sales Assistant: "*Hades* – this 100% pigskin leather jacket, was €99.95, is now 70% off – succumb to temptation."

DEFINITIONS

98% Cotton, 2% Elastane = Regular Fit Jeans

95% Cotton, 5% Elastane = Skinny Jeans

The difference between being hip and being square is 3% elastane.

NAMES

- *Mystic*: top.
- *Tolerant*: top.
- *Egypt*: dress.
- *Rigolo*: top.
- *Jane*: jeans.
- *Tabata*: striped dress. Tabata was the *nom de cul* of a famous '90s porn star.
- *Martinique*: white linen trousers. In the days when slavery still existed in Martinique, the Béké overseers wore white linen trousers as they patrolled the sugar plantations.
- *Toronto*, *Denver*, *San Francisco*, *Dakar*: dresses. In the geography of the Camaïeu outlet, Dakar is next to San Francisco.

JEANS

A pair of jeans named *Jane*.

THE "NAMERS"

Somewhere amid the thousands of pages dealing with apparel, on a Camaïeu Company Chart, there exists the position of "namer": those specialised in christening dresses and trousers of every sort.

THE "NAMERS" 2

The security guard imagines a work session involving three "namers".

The three women are seated at a table, each holding a flute of champagne; a silver bucket of caviar is within spoon-reach. Garments on hangers swish past on a motorised steel rail. A floral print dress appears. Between two sips of Veuve Clicquot, a "namer" solemnly intones: "Your name shall be *Hibiscus*, I have willed it so. Next!" The other two nod gravely, mouths filled with sturgeon roe. Another dress glides into view.

VISCOSE VIRTUOSOS

· *Hummingbird, Rock Lobster, Tapir*: respectively 92%, 95% and 98% viscose ... The greater the concentration of viscose, the more inclined the "namers" are to name the garments after endangered species.

RADIO CAMAÏEU 3

Radio Camaïeu croons softly into the ears of an old woman who gently sways her hips and nods her head as she rummages through dresses marked 70% OFF – the highest discount to date.

"%". Like a cock nestled between a pair of balls, the symbol "%", printed on the countless banners that hang from the false ceiling, hovers above the heads of all these women aroused by sale prices.

POLYMER

Polyester, polyamide, polyvinyl chloride … these are substances or materials consisting of very large synthetic molecules and are used in the textile industry. Scientists refer to them as polymers.

With motherhood behind them and their sex lives on the wane, women over fifty are particularly drawn to polyester, polyamide and polyvinyl chloride. The security guard calls them "polysisters".

HIDE-AND-SEEK

Beware the security guard who is, or appears to be, bored.

To pass the time, the security guard will sometimes play hide-and-seek.

The security guard hides from the shoplifter, hoping to catch her *in flagrante delicto*. The shoplifter hides from the security guard so as not to be caught red-handed.

The shoplifter must expend an inordinate amount of time simply to make off with a €20.95 pair of shoes discounted by 30%. After two hours of cat and mouse, should the thief have pulled off her petty larceny, she still has to factor in the time it takes to sell her plunder for about half the retail price, at best. Given the risks involved, the skills required and an average of three hours between theft and resale, it seems fair to say that "Camaïeu shoplifter" is not exactly a lucrative profession.

HIDE-AND-SEEK 2

Playing hide-and-seek among the rails of evening dresses is the favourite pastime of restless children.

THE TEENAGER IN THE WHEELCHAIR 2

The father helps the teenage girl out of the chair and walks her to the changing rooms. Hands gently cradle bodies, arms weave, intertwine, embrace, support... There is a great tenderness between the father and his daughter. They are bound both by filial affection and by the girl's physical dependency. In truth, each is supporting the other. Dependency is not always where we imagine it to be. Do those

35

compelled to touch so often develop a gentleness, a tenderness above the average? Would we be gentler towards each other if we touched more often?

THE BLIND WOMAN

Accompanied by her husband, her daughter and her dog, a blind woman is doing the sales. The man chatters to her constantly; his accent is from somewhere in the South of France, and he speaks in precise, carefully constructed sentences. She spends time stroking the fabrics in order to make her choice. From time to time, he gently places his hand on hers to steer her in the right direction. Another couple compelled to touch. Another display of tenderness. Another relationship based on co-dependency. The woman's disability enhances the communication of those around her.

THE TEENAGER'S WHEELCHAIR: TECHNICAL SPECIFICATIONS

- Two powered front wheels;
- Electric motor;
- Large lithium-ion battery;
- Moulded fluorescent-green headrest to keep the spine straight;
- Ingenious system of storage spaces to either side and beneath the seat;

- Directional joystick with a mini-LCD monitor mounted on the right-hand armrest;
- Around the joystick, four buttons, one with a trumpet icon.

Does this teenager's wheelchair foreshadow the cars of the future? It is a far cry from the board mounted on four wheels used long ago by polio victims and amputees.

SECURITY GUARD: BIOMECHANICS

By what paradox of biomechanics does the security guard invariably suffer from an aching coccyx when he spends his whole day on his feet?

SECURITY GUARD: BIOLOGY

Tenesmus. The Incontinent Urge ... The powerful need to micturate one hour before his break.

SPEAKING IN TONGUES

A large sign mounted on the back wall of the shop reads: SALDI, ZĽAVY, SOLDEN, ÁRLESZÁLLÍTÁS, WYPRZE-DAŻ, SLEVY, АКЦИЯ, REDUCERI, PROMOTIONALE, REBAJAS ... Europe, too, is built on consumerism.

ÉLISABETH

Élisabeth is a sales assistant who looks disturbingly anorexic, being thirty-two kilos and five foot six. She is not backward in coming forward and never misses an opportunity to wink or flash a smile at the security guard, who weighs about a hundred kilos. The natural attraction of polar opposites.

ÉLISABETH 2

Before heading home, the security guard will hand out Carambar® sweets to all the Camaïeu salesgirls. Élisabeth will get two.

WHEN THE MUSIC STOPS

7.30 p.m. The music stops.

The metallic clang of clothes hangers sliding along display rails: the shop assistants are clearing up. The straggling customers are clearing out. With polite but firm platitudes, the security guard must steer them towards the checkout counters, all the while ensuring that no new customers sneak in. This is his grand finale: doing the splits. Inside, there is always someone swearing on her mother's life that she will only be two minutes. At the door, there is always someone swearing on her mother's life that she will only need two minutes. The security guard is eyed with contempt when he refuses to grant these two-minute stays of execution. It is difficult to accept being snubbed by those one never notices. Here, everything is on sale, even self-esteem.

THE BRONZE AGE:
1960–1980

As he headed down the boulevard Vincent-Auriol towards the Seine, Ferdinand was thinking that he was sick and tired of the hypocritical "groupies". This is the term he'd come up with for students in the residence who constantly convened group meetings to talk about everything and decide on nothing. Yesterday, it was to discuss "the appropriate measures to be instigated" regarding the "inexcusable attitudes of the Embassy of Côte d'Ivoire", which had decided that it would no longer provide free toilet paper to the residence. After three hours in conclave, they had still not agreed on the wording of the "motion of censure" to be hand-delivered to the Ambassador's office at 102 avenue Raymond-Poincaré. The "communist" group disputed every jot and tittle with the "socialist sell-outs". The "liberalists", those "seditious lackeys of imperialism and flunkies of global capital", risked being lynched whenever they voiced an opinion. When, after two hours of spluttered insults and invectives, they finally came to the end of the first paragraph, the "communists" started to tear into each other because the "Chinese tendency" considered the "Russian tendency" too mealy mouthed, while the "Albanians", who could not stand the sight of the "Chinese", accused the "Russians" of being smug and condescending. This morning, although no action had yet been taken regarding the toilet paper imbroglio, another group meeting was convoked. "The Perspectives of African Intellectuals faced with the Consequences of the Oil Crisis" triggered incontinent bouts of logorrhoea and grandstanding for the rest of the day. The shrill whistle blasts that summoned delegates had sounded just before the old alarm clock that habitually woke Ferdinand. It was just as well, since he could not afford to be late for work.

Ferdinand was not a student. Had never been a student. Nonetheless, he lived at the RSCI[4] – the Residence for Students from Côte d'Ivoire. He had, after a fashion, inherited the room from his cousin André, who had gone home some months earlier with his diploma in medicine in his back pocket. In his heart of hearts, Ferdinand had always known that he would never equal the long and brilliant academic achievements of his cousin. As, doubtless, had

---

4 Author's note: On the boulevard Vincent-Auriol in Paris. Not to be confused with the RSSCI: the Revolutionary Society of Students from Côte d'Ivoire.

his teachers and probably his parents. And so, when, for the third time, he failed the CEPE to graduate from primary school, it took little to persuade his father to send him to France to "find himself". Ferdinand had sworn upon the family fetish that he would not come home until he had become a "big somebody". All the profits from the harvest of coffee beans and cocoa beans had gone to buy his plane ticket. One grey morning liberally moistened by the early showers of the rainy season in early October 1973, Ferdinand boarded a DC-10 sporting the green livery of Air Afrique. He became only the second man from his village to go to France.

André met Ferdinand at the RSCI in the little student bedsit he shared with Jean-Marie, a philosophy student and a veteran and irrepressible "groupie". Finding that the bursary he received was insufficient to allow him to survive in France and also to send money home to the large family he had left back in the home country, André had taken a part-time job working as a security guard at Les Grands Moulins de Paris, the old flour mills by the river. It was there, one morning, as the night shift was ending, that he saved an elderly worker who had suffered a heart attack and collapsed outside his little shelter. The rumour had spread through the factory. "That there Black security guard" had saved the life of Pierre-Alain Jacquinot, known to all as Pierrot, leader of the all-powerful branch of CGT union at Les Grands Moulins. It was at this point that they discovered that "that there Black security guard" was not called "hey, you!" but André, and had a parallel life studying to be a doctor at the Pierre and Marie Curie Faculty of Sciences at the Sorbonne. Most of those working in the flour mills saw little difference between someone studying to be a doctor and a doctor. As a result, from that day on, many came to him in secret to confess their aches and pains. Never had the "shelter" seemed so appropriately named. Indeed, more than a refuge, it became a veritable doctor's consulting room. André, unsurprisingly, was nicknamed "Doc". For years, he opened the factory gates as often as he had factory workers open their mouths and say "Aah". Often, he made appointments for them at the hospital where he practised. His fellow junior doctors at Pitié-Salpêtrière were always surprised by the number of people who looked for him or greeted him so warmly in the corridors. The factory workers felt close to the "African Doc". Was it simply a matter of distance? At Les Grands Moulins, the security shelter was next to the main factory building, whereas the sickbay was located on the fifth floor, surrounded by the offices of senior managers. It is easier to join a workplace on the factory floor. And, with all his connections among the workforce, André had no difficulty getting a job for his cousin. So, only two days after he arrived in France, Ferdinand was already working at Les Grands Moulins.

"For almost two years now, an eviction notice has been looming over the RSCI."

It was André who began. He had only just heard the news. And from a reliable source. He had been told by an elderly lawyer whose enlarged prostate he had treated that, for almost a decade now, the building at 150 boulevard Vincent-Auriol no longer belonged to Côte d'Ivoire. André was more inclined to believe this old White man than the claptrap served up by the Ivoirian Embassy every time the rumour prompted questions.

"In the early '60s, Houphouët-Boigny suffered an acute case of coup-d'étalgia," André continued, with his tendency to medicalise terminology. "He saw treachery in everyone and in everything: plots to assassinate or overthrow him, plots to snatch away the power he so cherished." With a swift gesture, André raised his beer glass to his lips, and when he set it down, half the liquid had been siphoned into his gullet.

"It all began in early 1959 with a benign paranoid growth, when, as President-elect, he exposed the famous 'Black Cat Conspiracy'. With a completely straight face, Houphouët-Boigny announced to the whole world that a political rival had attempted to assassinate him using vodou by burying a black cat in the local cemetery. Apparently, a photograph of him had been found stitched inside the bowels of the defunct domestic felid. At first, like ageing hyenas sated on spoiled meat, everyone laughed. Besides, you should have seen his face. I thought he was finding it difficult not to burst out laughing himself as he recounted the convoluted story to the foreign and domestic press, especially when it came to reading the cabalistic phrases inscribed on the back of the photograph found among the entrails of the black cat. But he was deadly serious. He dispatched an elite police squad specially trained in warding off evil spells and malevolent marabouts. They quickly arrested all those who were alleged to have hatched the sinister plot, among them my old friend Jean-Baptiste Mockey, who was charged with personally formulating the mysterious hex. Granted, Jean-Baptiste was a pharmacist, but the real problem was that, within the party, he was beginning to overshadow big chief Boigny. He was imprisoned in the cellars of the presidential palace, right below the office of the president. Luckily, by that time, I was in France; otherwise, like Jean-Baptise and all those who criticised the bourgeois attitudes of the old guard, I would have had a taste of prison slops."

André paused to quaff the rest of his beer and immediately ordered another. Angela Yohou was staring into her cup of tea. From time to time, Ferdinand would give her a sidelong glance, all the while trying to seem engrossed by André, who was now in full flight.

"Then, in January 1963, when the President of Togo, my friend Sylvanus Olympio, was assassinated by a young sergeant named Eyadéma, Houphouët-Boigny's benign paranoid growth metastasised into full-blown coup-d'étalgia. The image of poor Sylvanus's corpse sprawled in the courtyard of the US Embassy in Lomé, wearing nothing but a pair of shorts, his bare chest riddled with bullet holes, was a serious exacerbating factor. A few days after the tragedy in Togo, Houphouët claimed to have thwarted the 'Young Men's Coup'. Upshot: everyone around the age of thirty with a promising career in the administration was arrested. He locked them up in Assabou, a prison he had built near his native village, so that he and his elderly sister Faitai could personally keep an eye on the enemies he had succeeded in unmasking using a plethora of gris-gris, zealous informants and the numerous French military advisors who protected him.

"In August of the same year, the 'Trois Glorieuses' – a three-day popular uprising – ousted Fulbert Youlou, defrocked priest and authoritarian president of Congo-Brazzaville. Independent Africa was barely three years old, and already there had been several military coups. But this was the first time that a popular uprising had ousted one of the Fathers of Independence. In place of the defrocked Abbot, the people installed Marien Ngouabi, one of the dictator's former comrades. When Houphouët-Boigny got wind of this, his coup-d'étalgia became positively necrotic. This time, he invented the 'Old Men's Coup'. Another batch of experienced administration officials – many of them his former brothers-in-arms – were rounded up and crammed into his private jail in Assabou. Ernest Boka, the former president of the Supreme Court, was found hanging from the chain of a flush toilet. Suicide, according to the police. Assassination, according to opposition leaders. It was during this period that Houphouët-Boigny arranged to sell the building at 150 boulevard Vincent-Auriol to one of his friends, an estate agent. As far as he is concerned, there are no students at the RSCI now. He believes the place to be a hideout for dangerous conspirators, die-hard communists and embittered pseudo-revolutionaries recruited by the secret services of eastern European countries. And the great Houphouët-Boigny is not about to use government money, i.e. his own money (or his own money, i.e. the treasury coffers) to pay for the upkeep of deadbeat dissidents intent on taking his power. The RSCI is finished. They're planning to throw everyone out onto the street."

Even though Ferdinand sometimes had trouble following his cousin's train of thought, he loved the fact that André talked to him like an equal. It made him feel proud and kindled a sense of self-confidence that he was sorely lacking. At the residence, only André and Angela spoke to him like this. The others did not even deign to answer when, his curiosity piqued, he asked questions about the incomprehensible theories they spouted all day long.

As André concluded his peroration, Angela, with troubling tenderness, took Ferdinand's hands in hers and, looking him in the eye, spoke to him in that familiar, warm, passionate voice.

"Ferdinand, you'll be staying here on your own. I'm going back to Abidjan on the same flight as André. I don't want my child to be born here, far from his family, far from his ancestors. I don't want to do what others do: have children here so that, as adults, they can get French passports. *Jus soli* – the right of soil. Why should such children give a damn about French soil, when their own soil – the land of their ancestral spirits – is still in the hands of the French and their African puppets? When Aké finishes his thesis, he can come back if he wants. I am leaving. But I know that you want to stay here, and that's good, because it is a choice that you've made. A life choice. You're not a hypocrite like the others at the residence. You are a good person. Never forget your true nature, your African nature, your courageous, compassionate nature. Work hard and save what you can. As soon as you've saved enough money, move out of the RSCI and send for your fiancée, Odette."

The vast Pitié-Salpêtrière Hospital loomed at the far end of the boulevard Vincent-Auriol. Ferdinand admired the courage it had taken for his cousin André to alternate between curing the ill and securing the mills. He walked slowly, thinking how fortunate he was not to have to take the métro to get to work. It was unnatural to descend into the bowels of the Earth in order to travel. In his village, only dead men and evil spirits dwelled underground. Tchétchet Ghéhi Lagô Tapê, father of all the gods, had abandoned the underworld to his evil cousin, Digbeu Téti Gazoa, lord of shadows. Through his childhood, Ferdinand had listened to terrifying stories about Koudouhou, the kingdom of the dead, the pestilential core of the Earth, the demonic lair of Gazoa. Having been seized by panic on the first occasion he took the métro, Ferdinand could not help but feel a fleeting shudder each time he took the steps that led down into its dark depths. Accordingly, he particularly enjoyed the walk to work at Les Grands Moulins. He always took the same route. His feet could make the journey unaided while he allowed his mind to wander through memories and reflections. Whenever Ferdinand recalled the dramatic farewell scene when André and Angela left the RSCI, he realised that, had he been White, his cheeks would have flushed every shade of red that day. He missed them both.

There were more and more "illegals" like Ferdinand living at the residence. Accordingly, there were fewer and fewer "real" students. Perennial university dropouts, the very "groupies" so prompt to offer grand moral lessons to the world at large now clung as tenaciously to their student rooms as – to quote Jean-Marie – "capitalist dogs" to "the colossal fortunes made on the broken backs of the working proletariat". No-one could now remember what it was the long-standing residents had come to France to study in the first place. But whatever it was, thought Ferdinand, they were very gifted at economics and business ventures of all kinds. They had established a lucrative business subletting student rooms, which was one of the reasons that the RSCI had become overcrowded and diverse. There was much friction and tension between "legals" and "illegals", between "renters" and "lodgers". In the early summer of 1974, the atmosphere in the residence was as toxic as the atmosphere in France.

The changes to the France that Ferdinand had encountered barely nine months earlier had been as swift as the jet plane that had brought him to the gleaming new airport named in honour of Charles de Gaulle, the most famous White man in all the villages of francophone Africa. This was "The Crisis". A serious crisis whose earliest intimations were clear from the frantic frequency with which politicians and journalists throughout the country used the noun phrase "The Crisis". The moment a microphone appeared, the moment a camera whirred into action, the moment a piece of paper flaunted the white of its cellulose, someone mentioned "The Crisis".

The Crisis had begun precisely one week after Ferdinand's arrival. The Arabic countries within OPEC announced that they would no longer sell oil to anyone. They said that they would rather leave the black gold to rot beneath the feet of their camels than sell it off for the price of a handful of dried dates when all the world understood its importance. Panic in the West.

"Thinking about all their factories, all the power stations, the plastic, the cars, the petrol stations, the clothes, the wigs, the supersonic planes, the fishing lines, the dayglo-orange sofas, the TVs etc., the West – led by America – was scared. Really scared. Scared it wouldn't have a refrigerator at home. Shit-scared. And, as so often happens when people are shit-scared, their sphincters give way and *splat* . . . The Crisis was born."

Using his customary medical metaphors, André had given Ferdinand a long and detailed explanation of how and why "La Crise" had put an end to the "Trentes Glorieuses", the thirty years of boom and full employment. But Ferdinand had not really understood. He always needed to translate concepts into concrete reality. The Crisis was responsible for many misfortunes that Ferdinand saw little sign of on the beautiful Paris streets he so loved to stroll. Though he paid close attention, it seemed to him the streets were just as clean, still swept by his Malian brothers; his

Arabic cousins still spent their days juddering behind pneumatic drills on the countless construction sites from which buildings bloomed as quickly as mushrooms after a rainy night; the branches of "Félix Potin" and "Prisunic" were just as full of foodstuffs and useless fripperies; the lines at the checkout desks were just as long; the smoking carriage in the métro was just as crammed, the air blue with overalls and smoke; the advertising hoardings and their imperious entreaties to conspicuous consumption were still the most visible embellishments in the city . . . No, Ferdinand could not seem to see "The Crisis" with his own eyes. But, as he usually did, he pretended to understand André's scholarly explanations. In fact, the only phrase he remembered was the "Trente Glorieuses". It had a wonderful ring, and it reminded him of the "Trois Glorieuses" revolution by the people of the Congo. Ferdinand simply thought that the French had somehow prolonged their glory for a lot longer than the Congolese.

When he reached the end of the boulevard, Ferdinand turned right onto the quai François-Mauriac. The Seine was now on his left. Its dark, tranquil waves seemed as unsettling as that of the Gbô-kada, the river in his village. It was forbidden to bathe in the waters of the Gbô-kada. Evil spirits had long since taken up residence there when Briba Mapê, nephew of the great god, had banished them from the village of men. After a few minutes' walk, the Tolbiac Bridge appeared. A barge passing between its spindly legs trailed a wake of spume across the Seine that would surely have displeased the age-old tenants of the Gbô-kada.

51

*

Pompidou, the president of France, died a few months after "The Crisis" began. People said he had been ill; the "oil shock" had probably finished him off. All the presidents from francophone Africa attended the funeral. In Notre-Dame, during a Catholic ceremony organised by the secular Republic of France, Jean-Bédel Bokassa I, self-proclaimed "Emperor" of the Central African Empire, loudly shed every tear in his body. Yes, this man who, without turning a hair, had murdered countless rivals while torturing the more fortunate and imprisoning them in squalid dungeons; this man sobbed his heart out for the television cameras. Anyone would have thought he had lost his own father. The Bété people would have praised him for being such a skilled mourner and so powerfully expressing his grief. The Akan people would have scolded him since they believe it is unseemly to cry more loudly than family of the deceased. But in Paris, the unanimous opinion about Bokassa's behaviour could be summed up in a single word: "madness!" Africans living in Paris were indignant. The residents of the RSCI were outraged. To the very core of their being. As always, a group meeting was convened to draft a letter of protest and indignation to the Central African diplomatic representatives. In fact, the "groupies" decided to go so far as to agree a "joint motion" with all the other African students in Paris. That would make people sit up and take notice. The Ivoirian contingent was chosen to host the powwow, dubbed the "pan-African symposium on the Bokassa affair". There were three initial reports before the summit meeting took place one Saturday in April. People flocked to the RSCI.

Their shoes spit-polished, their trousers belted at the chest, their jackets too big, their ties trailing down to their crotches, their necks and fingers bedecked with gold, their skin the burnished yellow of papaya (i.e., Black skin bleached with cortisone), the RCS[5] dispatched their most sartorially splendid members of La Sape. "Because the Residence of Congolese Students, the RCS, the temple of sapology, must, at all times and in all circumstances, be sapologically represented," as one of the Congolese delegates answered seriously when ironically asked whether he and his compatriots were attending a fancy dress ball. At 20 rue Béranger in the third arrondissement, in the midst of clothes shops run by Jewish traders, a stone's throw from the large branch of Tati on the place de la République, the RCS had become the *sanctum sanctorum* to a new religion: La SAPE, the Society of Ambiance-Makers and People of Elegance. These preening peacocks, incapable of locating the Sorbonne on a map of Paris, spent vast sums of money on opulent garments even as their residence – a magnificent five-storey Haussmann building bought by the Congolese taxpayer to afford a certain level of comfort to its most brilliant students – crumbled to become a cesspit barely fit for human habitation.

---

5 Author's note: Residence of Congolese Students.

There were also delegates from Ponia, the Residence of Students from West Africa. The Ponia was built on one of the "boulevards des Maréchaux" – the boulevard Poniatowski, hence its soubriquet. It was a remnant of the Great Colonial Exhibition of 1931. Overseas delegates, among them Léopold Sédar Senghor, member of parliament for the riding of Sénégal-Mauritanie, poet and founding member of the Négritude movement and president of Senegal, were billeted there. But the Ponia was now little more than a crumbling building on the outskirts of the bois de Vincennes. Given its prestigious past, a majority of those who lived there considered themselves the future poet-presidents of Africa. Had Senghor himself not sojourned with these walls, now bloated by the damp from an obsolete plumbing system? So, the "Poniacs" employed abstruse grammatical forms, bombastic rhetoric and poetic circumlocutions whose rules and usage they alone understood.

On the evening of the great "pan-African symposium on the Bokassa affair", Ferdinand was happy he had spent the night in the security shelter of Les Grands Moulins rather than wandering the halls of the RSCI. The factory operated 24/7 and Ferdinand spent eight hours a day, sometimes more, raising and lowering the security barrier. He also recorded the registration plates of all vehicles entering or leaving the site. He knew everyone now. But many of them, even colleagues he had been working shifts with for nine months, still referred to him as "Doc", like his cousin André. His roommate, Jean-Marie, told him, "To White people, all Blacks look alike". Ferdinand had long since stopped listening to Jean-Marie. He had no use for the wild ravings of a part-time philosophy student and full-time alcoholic.

He was not bothered that people took him for his brilliant cousin. He was not remotely embarrassed to be mistaken for André, even if he knew it stemmed from an assortment of racist clichés, inattention and intellectual laziness. No, it was not about the colour of his skin. The scant attention paid to him as he raised and lowered the barrier was linked to his role as a security guard. But to Ferdinand, that was not what mattered. What mattered were his new uniform and his new responsibilities: the shiny black shoes, the handsome blue uniform, the white peaked cap. For the first time in his life, he felt important. For the first time in his life, he was earning the money he needed by the sweat of his brow. For the first time in his life, he no longer had to rely on the goodwill of a "brother", an "uncle", an "aunt" or anyone else in the "family" in order to do what he wanted, when he wanted. That feeling of independence! Ferdinand would keep his promise to Angela. He would not lose his way. He would work hard. Now that André had gone back to the village, it was Ferdinand who sent back news from France. A month earlier, he had posed in his security guard's uniform and sent the photograph to Odette. The picture had done the rounds of every house in the village, apparently. Everyone thought he had become a police officer in the land of the White man.

*

On the quai Panhard-et-Levassor, the western elevation of Les Grands Moulins towered, with its unkempt thatch of black slate tiles. Vinous vapours drifted from the last wine warehouses of Bercy, swelled with moisture as they crossed the Seine and teased Ferdinand's nostrils with their acrid scent. He did not like the smell. The elections that had followed the death of Pompidou had exuded a miasma just as foul and acrid. The candidates in the presidential race were ten bald men, a man who was blind in one eye and a woman who could not have been uglier had she been bald and blind in one eye. Predictably, every one of them had the solution to "The Crisis". The slogan of the moment: "We've got no oil, but we've got ideas." One of these ideas was that there were too many foreigners in France. During "The Crisis", they were stealing jobs from true-born Frenchmen, snatching the bed from the pure or the bread from the poor. It was intolerable, especially coming from those with whom they had so kindly allowed to board the gravy train of the Trente Glorieuses. Intolerable. The presidency, therefore, would be conferred on whoever came up with the best "idea" to stem the tide of these hordes of thankless foreigners. The centre-right slaphead talked about "national preference". This "idea" appealed to many French people, especially the candidate who was blind in one eye and had the other firmly fixed on the far-right. It would later become his political warhorse. The left-wing slaphead talked about humanism and heart only to be swiftly put in his place by the centrist slaphead who, in front of a baying television audience, brusquely replied that he did not have a monopoly on the heart. As it happened, thanks to André and Angela, Ferdinand was already aware that the left-wing slaphead had been Minister for the Colonies. The Malagasy and Cameroonian survivors of the revolutions that had been brutally and bloodily suppressed still remembered his sense of humanism and heart. Ferdinand loathed hypocrites and was happy to see the balding left-wing bastard being publicly put in his place. It was this cardiological riposte that led to Giscard d'Estaing winning the presidential election in May. He appointed a man named Poniatowski as Minister of the Interior. Poniatowski immediately legislated to introduce "residence permits" to "deter" foreigners and signed a decree preventing family reunifications that would come into force the following summer. At the Ponia, there was talk of renaming the building. Others quickly pointed out that Giscard's minister was related by blood to Józef Poniatowski, the Polish general whom Napoleon appointed Marshal of France. In the sweltering rooms and squalid hallways of the Ponia, the air was thick with fine words and poetic phrases intended to censure this iniquitous decision taken by the descendant of immigrants.

"If this man is Frrrench today, it is because his Polish ancestor died defending Frrrance. Granted, he was shot in battle, but he was shot in the back, which means he was beating a retreat when hit by the enemy's bullet. But before he fled, he fought to defend the Frrrench Empire. We too have lost fathers beneath the tricolourr banners of the coq au vin. Our forefathers stood tall. They faced the flames and the hail of fire that threatened the motherland. They took the enemy's bullets in the chest so that eternal Frrrance might live," announced a Ponia resident from Benin, the Malraux quaver in his voice rippled by his obsession with rolling his Rs.

"And not just once, but twice!" agreed a Togolese resident from the audience.

"Never take a nap next to the house of an undertaker who has just learned his trade. Unlike those of us from Saint-Louis in Senegal, these people, this Poniatowski and his family, have not been French for long, which probably explains his zeal." This declaration by a resident from Senegal triggered murmurs of approval and much vehement nodding.

"One day, the son of an immigrant will be president of this country, and I am sure that he will be the one to drive all foreigners out of France," prophesied a resident from Mali.

"Poniatowski, eeech! A man with a name as unpronounceable as a Sri Lankan-born Azerbaijani has no business lecturing the sons of Senghor on what it means to be French," came the volte-face from a resident from Upper Volta.

There were also imprecations uttered in Djerma, the language of southwestern Niger. According to the speaker's Hausa neighbour, it had something to do with visiting haemorrhagic diarrhoea and atrophied testicles on the male line of the Poniatowski family until such time as the waters of the Niger flowed from the Atlantic Ocean to the Fouta Djallon mountains . . .

Despite their heartfelt denunciations, the students living in the Ponia, like those in all the Black university halls of residence in Paris, were careful not to miss their appointment at the prefecture so they could procure this new access-all-areas residence permit. Ferdinand, for his part, was surprised that a politician would so quickly keep his promise. The new laws regulating residency for foreigners were swiftly rushed through the Assemblée nationale by a multiparty vote which drew support from members from across the political spectrum. The "monopoly of the heart" had struck a chord with the political community. Meanwhile, those who did not meet the new criteria for residency were hardly having a gay old time. Overnight, a new class of citizen was created: the undocumented immigrant.

Fortunately, Ferdinand followed the advice of André and Angela to the letter. Odette was to arrive in just four days, a full two weeks before the new laws by Giscard's gang came into effect. Ferdinand had already found a decent apartment in which to welcome his fiancée when she arrived from the village. As he walked towards his security hut, he patted his coat pocket and felt the document he had signed only the night before: a rental agreement. He had leased a small apartment in the seventeenth arrondissement, on the rue La Condamine, next to the railway tracks of the gare Saint-Lazare. He felt as though he had been reborn. No more group meetings. No more traipsing down endless corridors in all weathers clutching a roll of toilet paper to go to the toilet. Taking the métro to work? He would get used to it. A bedroom, a living room, a kitchen, a shower and a toilet. Ferdinand would have a home to call his own. He had finally arrived in France, his France. He and his little Odette had decided to start a family. Being a security guard was a good job.

Ferdinand arrived at Les Grands Moulins.

A BRANCH OF
SEPHORA ON THE
CHAMPS-ÉLYSÉES

CHAMPS-ÉLYSÉES

Shops, boutiques, supermarkets, shopping malls, hotels, restaurant chains... If this truly is the most beautiful avenue in all the world, then the security guard is a florist-cum-fridge salesman-cum-thalassotherapist to the Inuit.

MIB

At the branch of Sephora on the Champs-Élysées, the security guard wears a black jacket, black trousers, black shirt, black tie. He is the MIB: the Man in Black. He works his shift with four others and a supervisor who sits behind a bank of monitors surveying footage from the forty cameras bristling around the boutique. He has a walkie-talkie connected to a transparent earpiece. A swanky guard for a swanky avenue.

$$J(N+1)$$

The MIBs at Sephora communicate with each other via the earpieces and track suspects or supposed shoplifters according to their morphotype, using codes that conform to the numerical sequence with the formula J(n+1), in which *n* is an integer.

J3: Arabic;

J4: Negroid;

J5: Caucasian;

J6: Asian.

The security guard does not dare ask what call signs should be used for persons of mixed ethnicity. J4/5 biracial Black and Caucasian? J3/6 Arab-Asian? J6/4 Black Asian . . . Given its high levels of interracial marriages and improbable combinations, the security guard cannot help but think that his counterparts in Brazil must have a much more complex formula to categorise people according to physical type. In Brazil, they say that God created man, and the Portuguese created mixed-race man.

WUO

Bathed as they are in so many mingled fragrances all day long, a woman who works as a sales assistant at Sephora becomes a WUO: Woman of Unidentifiable Odour.

MUSO

Like the sales assistant, the security guard is also bathed in perfume all day long. This makes him a MUSO: Man of Unidentifiable Security Odour.

FART

The security guard is always searching for an epithet to describe the mingled odours created when a stinking fart is unleashed in the women's perfume department.

SHOWER

"Walah! It smells so good. I'm never going to wash myself ever again!"

A tween, having literally doused herself with multiple bottles of perfume from the display.

Because of the free availability of test samples, the perfume shower is the most widely practised sport at

Sephora. It is not uncommon to see people simultaneously spray themselves with fragrances from every possible parfumier and simply walk out, euphoric and radiant.

SEPHORAAAA OR SEPHOOOORA

The branch of Sephora on the Champs-Élysées is one of the largest in the world. As they step inside, or sometimes simply walking past, people often shriek as though they've just spotted an old friend they are about to run to and embrace: *"Sephoraaaa!"* (version française) *"Oh my God! Sephoooora!"* (English version).

SEPHORAAAAARRGH

Outside, a carpet as red as a mammal's tongue. Stretching away, lines of pillars painted in black-and-white stripes; from a distance, they resemble rows of sharp teeth. The entrance to Sephora is the maw of a wild beast belching its pungent poly-perfumed breath onto the Champs-Élysées.

BAR

Gift Bar, Make-Up Bar, Brow Bar, Care Bar, etc. Then again, perfumes do have a high alcohol content.

AMY WINEHOUSE

One woman is the spitting image of Amy Winehouse. So much so that the security guard worries that, rather than spraying the perfumes on her skin, she will open them and swig from the bottles.

MECCA

With its mosque, its Islamic bookshops, its halal butchers, its shops selling clothes, hijabs and Islamic veils, the rue Jean-Pierre Timbaud in Belleville is known locally as Jalalabad.

Sephora is Mecca and, within it, the Christian Dior concession is the Ka'bah towards which all women turn, Arabic or otherwise, veiled or otherwise, in the name of the most holy perfume.

EMIR'S WIFE

Cloaked from head to toe in a black veil, her every step reveals a glimpse of a patent leather stiletto and an ankle encircled by the cuff of a pair of jeans that, one imagines, tightly hugs the rest of the leg. She is accompanied by a female servant, an aide and a bodyguard. They are easily recognisable from their roles. The servant, a young Filipina woman with a particularly pimply face, is carrying bags from every luxury emporium from the place Vendôme to the Champs-Élysées. The aide, a rather effeminate Arab man, has her handbag tucked under his arm and conspicuously holds the credit card between the index and middle fingers of his hand. The bodyguard is the man carrying three umbrellas who meekly trails after them.

SEPHOARABIA OR
THE DANCE OF THE VEILS

Whether French or foreign, Parisians or suburbanites, male or female, rich or poor, young or old, prole or prince, Sephora draws Arabs from all walks of life. This is the origin of the dance of the veils.

Whether black or coloured, single or multiple, transparent or opaque, short- or long-sleeved, faces covered or partially revealed, hijab can be worn in countless styles.

AMERICANOPHILES

An Arab couple. The husband wears a T-shirt printed with a map of the New York subway. The wife, fully veiled, is wearing a grey bubu with sleeves stitched from fabric printed like a ten-dollar bill. Clearly visible on her left elbow is the motto of the United States of America: "*In God We Trust*".

MIBS AND WIBS

At Sephora, the Men in Black are the security guards; the WIBs, the Women in Black, are those who wear the niqab. They could potentially make perfectly matched couples. *"Narcs and Niqabi of the world, unite!"*

BE ICONE

A WIB looking for a particular product is kneeling before the Dior concession. Above her head, a flickering publicity slogan: *"Dior addict, be Icone"*.

CONFUSION

From time to time, a WIB wearing the fullest fundamentalist veil slips a lipstick or eyebrow pencil beneath her niqab. The security guard is convinced he has caught a shoplifter red-handed . . . until he notices that, in her other hand, the WIB is holding a small mirror that also disappears beneath the veil. This is a Muslim makeover, a Niqab New Look.

FATHER-DAUGHTER

An Arabic father (Saudi, Kuwaiti, Qatari, Egyptian?) is playing with his daughter, tossing her up in the air and catching her. The little girl's hair flutters in the breeze; she is pretty and father and daughter are giggling loudly. They look so happy. The security guard cannot help but wonder whether this father will one day insist that his daughter wear the full veil.

THE SCHEHERAZADE THEORY

Thousands of years ago, hammams were the first beauty salons and wellness centres. Mascara, kohl, henna, argan oil, graphite, lip rouge, etc., the art of make-up as we know it today has its roots in Arabic culture. It was brought from the Orient by the crusaders, who must have been delighted to encounter women wreathed in intoxicating fragrances, their lustrous hair free of lice, their eyes delicately outlined, their cheeks powdered with something more becoming than flour. In the tales of the *One Thousand and One Nights*, Scheherazade is the quintessence of the beautiful, flirtatious woman. Today, she would be the perfect brand ambassador for L'Oréal or Christian Dior.

GOLF HANDICAP

Bahrain, Qatar, Kuwait, the United Arab Emirates, Saudi Arabia, regardless of physiognomy, every Arabic golfer from the Persian Gulf exhibits at least one sign of corpulence. One in two is clearly obese.

The bodies of the Bedouin, who, for millennia, have weathered harsh desert conditions, evolved to store what little food it could get for as long as possible. It was stored as reserves of fat in anticipation of long periods of scarcity. Such bodies were ill-prepared for the opulence and riches suddenly visited on them by the oil boom and the massive influx of petrodollars. Their food, now rich and plentiful, continues to be converted into fat and stored for long periods. It is impossible to undo in thirty years what it has taken nature more than three thousand years to perfect.

ALHAMDULILLAH

An Arab woman without a veil, bottle blonde, in full evening dress, emits a booming burp that is clearly audible above the ambient commotion. Then, seeing that the security guard has noticed, says, *"Alhamdulillah!"*

When Islam was first introduced to the Bedouin peoples, meals were so frugal that it was rare for them to produce a breath of wind. So, on the rare occasions when a meal produced an eructation, it was considered polite to express gratitude to Allah for this miracle.

FROM MALL TO MALL

Leaving Dubai, that city-cum-shopping-complex, to holiday in Paris and pick up a few essentials on the Champs-Élysées, that avenue-cum-shopping-mall.

Crude oil gives access to the wide world but narrows its horizons.

TALKING T-SHIRTS

The T-shirt seems to have become a fashionable means of communication. From torsos – with or without breasts – and/or from backs, phrases, words, slogans, sometimes veritable professions of faith, tongue-lash the world at large.

- *Pretty little thing*. Worn by a woman with long blonde hair, of Nordic appearance, who is six foot two and weighs at least 150 kilos.
- *Eagles don't fly with pigeons*. Worn by a young Black man with a gangsta-rap look. He sticks to his girlfriend like a leech.
- *She says no to boys*. Worn by a woman with impressive curves and an extravagant sway to her hips. If what's written on her T-shirt is true, the security guard knows a lot of African men who would send her to a marabout to have that spell lifted.
- *I'm dark but not gloomy*. Worn by a short, dark-skinned girl with cropped hair and a masculine gait.

- *Don't abuse alcohol, just drink it.* Worn by a tall blond guy who speaks a language that sounds vaguely Slavic.
- *I hit like a boy.* Worn by a Lilliputian Asian girl.
- *Bitch Betta Have My Money.* A poetic song from a badass Black rapper from Queens called Ja Rule and worn by a shortass White guy dressed like an '80s rapper.
- *Ici c'est Paris, fuck l'OM!* Worn by a fair-haired boy of about eleven accompanied by his young parents.

THE VEIL AND THE HOODIE

No-one is allowed to enter Sephora wearing a hoodie with the hood up. But it is certainly not forbidden to wear a veil, even a niqab. What approach should the security guard take when he sees a young woman coming in wearing a hoodie over her burqa?

ON THE NATURAL ATTRACTION OF POLAR OPPOSITES

A tall White guy, six foot ten, very pale with a bleach-blond mohawk, is holding the hand of a short, dark-skinned Black woman who cannot be more than four feet eleven. The woman is *heavily* pregnant, and this accentuates the impression of a butter ball next to a beanpole. The man stares straight ahead as he talks, never bowing his head. The woman answers without ever raising hers. Neither shouts, despite the yawning void that separates them. They must have phones with invisible earpieces to carry on a conversation like this. Otherwise, it would be impossible given the hullabaloo in the shop.

DIALOGUE

Panicked elderly woman, addressing the security guard: "Monsieur, Monsieur, I can't find my daughter. Could you please help me look for her?"

Security guard: "Can you tell me what she looks like, Madame?"

Elderly woman, now almost hysterical: "She's blonde, with short hair, her name is Marion and..."

Security guard: "Try to stay calm, Madame. We'll find her. I'll put a call out right now. How old is your daughter?

Elderly woman: "She's forty."

Security guard: "Madame, a forty-year-old woman can't get lost in a shop!"

Elderly woman, on the verge of tears: "You don't understand, Monsieur. I'm the one who's lost!"

TATTOO VS HENNA

On skins, the war between Tattoo and Henna is raging.

FRAGILE

As though on a cardboard box containing breakable items, a woman with short hair has had the word "Fragile" tattooed on the back of her neck, between C3 and C4. Entirely apt. C3 and C4 are the cervical vertebrae located at the base of the skull. They are very fragile. The slightest fracture could sever the spinal cord, resulting in irreversible paralysis or death from neurodegeneration.

BARCODES

A young girl has had a barcode tattooed on her neck. It's tempting to scan her with one of the infrared guns at the checkout to see how much she costs.

BLACK TATTOO

Because of the weak contrast between black of the tattooing ink and the skin, tattoos on Black people look more like dermatosis. Moreover, the natural tendency of Black skin to produce keloid scars means that, close up, Black people's tattoos are 3D.

NUDE FINISH FOUNDATION

Nude implies the colour of a person's skin before the application of foundation. So, what is "Nude Finish Foundation"? Curious concept.

WORDPLAY

The industry that trades in *beauté*,
   Is marked by heavy handed wordplay:

Dior: *J'adore*

Calvin Klein Obsession: *Between love and madness lies obsession*

Benefit: *The POREfessional*

Maybelline: *Maybe she's born with it. Maybe it's Maybelline...*

Diesel: *Fuel for Life...*

WHEN WORDS FAIL

Quoted *in extenso*:

Yes to tomatoes
Skin cream for creamy skin
Really Great

DIESEL: FUEL FOR LIFE

On the publicity poster, a beautiful young man, his lips parted, his shirt open to reveal his sculpted torso. The perfume bottle seems to protrude from the open flies of his jeans. Like a tumescent phallus on a single bulbous testicle.

DIALOGUE

Thirty-something woman to her fascinated girlfriend: "He said he was bi, but personally I thought it was because he hadn't dealt with the fact that he's gay."
The friend: "And then what?"
The woman, with an unmistakable arm gesture: "He had a huge hard-on."
The friend: "Nooo . . . ! And then what?"
"And then he jumped me like he just got out of prison."
"Nooooo!"
The two women laugh heartily. They are standing in front of the poster for "Diesel: Fuel for Life".

TCHATCHO AND KPAKPATO

Tchatcho is a word used to describe those Africans, male or female, who artificially lighten their skin. These "neophyte Whites", these "chiaroscuros" are invariably betrayed by those parts of the anatomy that resist "whitening": the joints of the wrist and hand. Consequently, these parts of the body are called *Kpakpato* – traitors.

The security guard thinks he has spotted a Tchatcho woman, but she is cunningly wearing gloves, making it impossible to categorically rule on the origins of the extreme pallor of her complexion compared to her Bantu features . . . Then suddenly, a ten-year-old boy appears behind her; he looks exactly like her. But his complexion is coal black. The Tchatcho is unmasked.

Moral: progeny can be an excellent Kpakpato for unmasking a Tchatcho.

THE "G" SPOT

The Tchatcho is wearing a pink velvet tracksuit. The brand is emblazoned in glittering faux diamonds on her buttocks: Christian Audigier. The long cursive tail of the "G" circles her arsehole like a target.

FLOKO

A White woman comes into the store carrying a bag on which is printed a large red colonial fez.

In French Colonial Africa, colonial guards or "gardes-de-cercle" were brutish, moronic Africans who were cruel and zealous in carrying out the orders of their White masters.

In Bambara, the word "Floko" means a little bag. The foreskin, which looks like a little bag at the end of the penis, is also called a "floko". Metonymically, the word is used to refer to those who are uncircumcised. In countries where circumcision is often a rite of passage, an initiation into adulthood and personal and collective responsibility, being called uncircumcised is particularly insulting. Loathed by the people for their brutality and their abuse of power, the gardes-de-cercle were nicknamed "floko guards". They each wore a red fez.

FLOKO 2

In his handsome red fez, the Negro used to advertise Banania cocoa powder is a floko guard! Behind his beaming smile, he hides a truncheon carved from iroko, the hardest wood in the forest, painted with whitewash so that it is visible at a distance, and as a reminder of the colour of the skin of the man who gave orders to bring it down on a head, a back, an arse. This may explain why cocoa powder was never as popular in the colonies as it was in metropolitan France.

FLOKO 3

A Black man with a pronounced American accent asks the security guard where he can find the Guerlain store. He is carrying a bag with the logo "Comptoir des Cotonniers". In other times, this man would have been an Uncle Tom, a less violent, but more zealous American counterpart to the floko guard.

WHITE LIPSTICK

A Black woman is applying white lipstick. It makes her look as though her lips are infected and filled with pus.

COLOUR CODES

The Sephora store is long and narrow, and the black-and-white striped pillars are reminiscent of a basketball referee. To the right, colour-coded orange, Men's Fragrances. To the left, colour-coded pink, Women's Fragrances. To the rear, colour-coded green, Face and Body Care. This zone is nicknamed "The Prairie", as much for its colour as because of the luxury Swiss skincare brand, La Prairie, which sells the most expensive item in the store: a "caviar cream" that costs €900 for 100 ml.

A COW IN THE PRAIRIE

A woman of tall stature with enormous breasts, buttocks and thighs is wearing a figure-hugging outfit of mottled black and white. Her septum piercing, a large nose ring, dangles over her upper lip as she chews gum and stares intently at a jar of La Prairie Skin Caviar.

THE LAUGHING COW

Needless to say, there are slightly more demanding jobs in security. The retail security guard is to the security industry what "The Laughing Cow" is to cheese.

HUGUENOT VENUS

An imposing steatopygous White woman with a china-doll face bears an astounding likeness to the famous Hottentot Venus. Had there been more White women like her, poor Saartjie Baartman would never have been turned into a freak show attraction in the odious human zoos of the nineteenth century. She would not have ended her life on a dissecting table in the National Museum of Natural History in Paris.

BIG CHIHUAHUA AND SMALL HUMAN

An elderly man steps into the boutique leading a giant chihuahua and a small human on leashes. The dog wears its leash around its neck. The child wears it around his waist. Noting the stunned expression on the face of the security guard, the elderly man winks and whispers:

"He's my grandson; he's hyperactive. I've got a medical certificate."

FOR WHOM THE
METAL DETECTOR TOLLS

The walk-through metal detector tolls when anyone enters or leaves with an item that has not been demagnetised. It signals only hypothetical guilt and, in 90 per cent of cases, the item has been duly paid for. But it is striking to note that almost everyone heeds the command of the security gate. Hardly anyone is insubordinate. However, reactions differ according to culture or nationality.

- The Frenchman looks around, as though someone else is responsible for this noise and he merely looking for the culprit in the spirit of collaboration.
- The Japanese customer stops dead and waits for the security guard to approach.
- The Chinese shopper does not, or pretends she does not, hear and continues on her way as nonchalantly as possible.

- The French citizen of Arabic or African ancestry accuses the device of conspiracy or racial profiling.
- The African jabs a finger at his chest as though seeking confirmation.
- The American rushes over to the security guard with a broad smile and all bags open for inspection.
- The German takes a step back in order to check that the system is functioning correctly.
- The Gulf Arab adopts a lofty, supercilious expression and slowly stops.
- The Brazilian puts his hands in the air.
- Once, a man actually fainted. He was unable to confirm his nationality.

THE FARADAY CAGE

The best way to evade the electromagnetic waves of the security gate and, hence, the security guard, is to place stolen articles in a Faraday cage. A homemade Faraday cage can easily be made by lining a bag with one or more layers of aluminium foil. This, however, can make the bag more rigid and the trained eye of the security guard may notice the deception. When in doubt, the security guard may trigger the alarm himself, thereby allowing him to search the bags of those who use Michael Faraday's scientific inventions rather than their personal debit cards when shopping.

DIOR *J'ADORE*

This perfume exerts a powerful magnetic attraction on Arabic, Chinese and Eastern European women. The boutique runs an informal daily sweepstake about the buyers of Dior *J'adore*. Yesterday, the grand prize went to United Arab Emirates, for a woman who had €1,399.76 worth of Dior *J'adore* in a shopping basket that came to a total of €3,456.85.

DIOR *J'ADORE* 2

A small head perched atop a long neck encircled by a stack of copper rings: the design of the Dior *J'adore* bottle evokes the famous "giraffe women" of Thailand. These women of the Kayan tribe, originally from Myanmar (formerly Burma), are packed into bogus authentic villages by tour operators where they are paraded for Western tourists for preposterous sums of money. With its "giraffe bottles", Dior *J'adore* hovers between rank cynicism and vain aestheticism.

THE SPOTLIGHT

Five or six times a day, the sales assistants form a guard of honour at the entrance. The music is cranked up to full volume and they all dance and clap their hands, keeping more or less to the beat. With Sephora, this is known as "the spotlight". It is one of the great attractions of the avenue des Champs-Élysées. Crowds gather outside the store to watch. Those customers who walk the red carpet at such times feel like celebrities, like stars. The most pitiful attempt at a dance step is greeted by wild cheering from the male and female sales assistants. Needless to say, everyone takes out their smartphone in order to immortalise this "memorable" moment. From a distance, it looks like a forest of camera phones mounted on human tripods. They watch the "performance" live streamed on their phones.

THE SPOTLIGHT 2

Far too many people, far too much noise, dreadful dancers, abysmal music, "the spotlight" is one of the most gruelling moments for the security guard.

Who will burn in hell for this particular piece of Global Popular Music?

Meanwhile, a curse upon David Guetta and the Black Eyed Peas.

DEODORANT

The perfect deodorant would be one used literally to obliterate all bodily odour. Not to replace it with another.

NIKON VS CANON

Asian tourists sporting huge cameras fitted with gargantuan lenses slung over their bellies can be divided into two groups:
- Yellow: black-and-yellow Nikon strap.
- Red: black-and-red Canon strap.

THE SHOE CARRIER

A young Japanese man enters with a Prada bag slung over his shoulder and, in one hand, dangling from a carabiner, a plastic gadget on which hangs a pair of visibly worn trainers: this is a Zpurs shoe carrier. The man is currently wearing a pair of blue sandals and the security guard imagines him performing a quick change when it starts to rain, shrieking "*banzai!*" When we do not understand "the other", we invent it, usually with racist clichés.

THE LV CULTURAL REVOLUTION

Belts, wallets, scarves, handbags, travel bags, suitcases, etc. Chinese customers invariably have at least one Louis Vuitton accessory. Mao's cultural revolution has reached its acme on the place Vendôme.

CHINA VS JAPAN

- Aside from the obligatory Louis Vuitton accessory, the Chinese customer dresses like Dédé or Henriette from the local sports bar next to the train station in La Ferté-sous-Jouarre[6] or Ambléon-sur-Gland[7].
- The Japanese customer dresses like Félix or Anne-Sophie from Le Chat Noir or Chez Prune in the swankier areas of Oberkampf or the Canal Saint-Martin.
- In conversation, the Chinese use a preponderance of "a" phonemes. China is a continental country, and therefore open, in a certain sense.
- In conversation, the Japanese use a preponderance of "o" phonemes. Japan is an island country and, therefore, insular.
- The Chinese always travel in groups.
- The Japanese often come in alone or in twos at the very most.
- The Chinese customer shouts, even when asking the security guard for information.
- The Japanese customer whispers, especially when asking the security guard for information.

---

6 Author's note: A small town in Seine-et-Marne, in the far-flung easterly suburbs of Paris where most employment is to be found at the vast shopping mall or the toll booth on the A4 autoroute.
7 Author's note: A village in Ain, north of Lyon, where quiet flows the Gland.

PARDON?

Like the Chinese, many Italians seem to be hard of hearing. How else to explain the fact that they talk so loudly when they are only inches from one another?

MESSIAH

"Art will save the world" Fyodor Dostoevsky

Printed in large letters on the handbag of an elderly lady.

SIGHTLESS, STATELESS CAPITAL

A woman enters wearing a full veil. There is not even an opening for her eyes. She could be in any country in the world. Printed in red on the bag she is carrying:

REVENUE
The Best Dividend Stocks
& Income Investments

NILOUFAR, THE PERSIAN GIRL

A sales assistant of Iranian heritage. She compensates for a rather unprepossessing face with a flawless, infectious smile. She radiates joie de vivre. Niloufar, in Farsi, translates as "Nymphaea" or "Water Lily". Certain species of lotus are Nymphaeaceae.

POOR TASTE

The young people from the poor banlieues, who are arbitrarily and abusively referred to as chavs or scum, go to the Hugo Boss concession to perfume themselves or to the Paco Rabanne stand to spray themselves with *1 Million*, which comes in a bottle shaped like a gold ingot. There are dreams in symbols and symbols in dreams.

RELEGATION

The Camaïeu axiom – "*In a clothing store, a customer without a bag is a customer who will not shoplift*" – does not hold good at Sephora. This, *ipso facto*, relegates the axiom to the status of mere theorem.

At Sephora, underpants, bras, pockets, clutch bags, scarves, baseball caps, gloves, baby buggies, in fact, anything that can be worn on the human body or used to transport small human bodies is susceptible to being used as a cache or a means of concealing an item that has not made the requisite stop at the cash register.

THE GOLDEN AGE:
1990–2000

Send money back to the old country. The woman wore a length of fabric knotted around her head. Her vivid, bright-coloured camisole was cut from the same material as her scarf. Clearly a "Dutch wax"[8] print. Possibly a "My-Man-Left-Me", a "The-Other-Woman-Be–Jealous" or a "Joined-At-The-Hip". Garish colours, strange patterns, picturesque names: no-one has ever seen a Dutch woman wearing this fabric. In Amsterdam and in Feyenoord, with the exception of Queen's Day, when everyone wears orange, Dutch clothing is as sober and sombre as it is across the rest of Europe. And yet, for generations, African women have sworn by this colourful "Wax Véritable, 100% made in Nederland".

---

8 Author's note: Double-printed cotton fabric common throughout West Africa. The pieces are made using the wax-based Indonesian technique called *batik* which was brought to Africa by Ghanaian soldiers who fought alongside the Netherlands in Java and Sumatra.

A "full piece" – twelve yards – costs as much as the monthly salary of a minor civil servant in Ouagadougou or Lomé.

The woman was captured with a broad smile surmounted by plump cheeks that shone in spite of her dark complexion. Her neck, descending in a gentle arc, broadened to become twin rounded shoulders. Her collarbones, ashamed to break this symphony of curves, created no hollows at the base of her throat. Only her breasts, which seemed monumental, dared intimate the beginnings of a groove, which was modestly covered by her precious Dutch wax fabric. The woman exuded heartiness and happiness; the picture wanted there to be no doubt on this point.

Send money back to the old country. The child stood next to the woman. He, too, was wearing a patterned shirt. Probably a "fancy fabric". Children's shirts are not made from Dutch wax fabric. It is simply not done. For children, "fancy is better!" Fancy is a fabric of inferior quality for everyday use. Fancy! With a name like this, the fabric probably had its origins in England's textile mills. Liverpool? Manchester? Perhaps. These days, fancy is manufactured in local factories in Bouaké or Abidjan. And in people's minds, this alone is enough to find all manner of imperfections in it, real or imagined. People say that fancy patterns faded more quickly than wax. But since it costs much less, it is worn more often and therefore washed more often. Slapped against a rock, vigorously scrubbed on wooden washboards, rinsed thoroughly, brutally mangled to squeeze out every last drop of water, then dried in the blazing tropical sun: what fabric could withstand such treatment? The boy's fancy shirt had clearly not yet suffered the forceful assaults of the "Fanico", the washer men. These muscular men toured local villages every morning in search of fabric to mistreat in the name of cleanliness and hygiene. In the photograph, the boy's shirt is new and immaculately pressed. No "Fanico" had ever put his hands on it. The child stared into the lens, his laughing eyes pulled into an almond shape by a smile as broad and beaming as the woman's. His tubby body and rounded face suggested a close kinship with the woman. Mother and son? Very likely. Certainly, the billboard was keen that there be no doubt on this point.

Send money back to the old country. On the billboard, the photograph was tucked into one of those wallets with a clear plastic compartment designed to hold snapshots of those people who are as close to one's wallet as to one's heart. Just below the photo, a large brown thumb made it clear that the wallet belonged to a Black man. Not a West Indian, otherwise his wife would be wearing an extravagant scarf, and the fabric would be chequered. Not an American, otherwise his wife would be wearing a lustrous black mane of hair extensions with eyes that were contact-lens-green and an elegant monochromatic pantsuit. No, the man holding this wallet was clearly an African. The clothes of the woman and the child left no room for doubt. Textile as a signifier of Africanness. The publicist was clearly well versed in the lexicon of clichés. Moreover, the geographical suffix "to the old country" proved he or she was intimately acquainted with the Pocket Dictionary of Pidgin French.

The slogan was printed at the bottom of the flyer in black type on a yellow background. Western Union® sang the praises of its money transfer service on a billboard four metres by three. *Send money back to the old country*. From his cramped security hut in what had once been Les Grands Moulins de Paris, Ossiri stared up at the twelve square metres of advertising.

On the quai Panhard-et-Levassor, Les Grands Moulins was now no more than an empty shell. For donkey's years, not a single gram of flour had been produced in the ghostly building wedged between the Seine and the railway tracks of the gare d'Austerlitz. To prevent dropouts and homeless people from squatting, the building was patrolled by security guards twenty-four hours a day, 365 days a year. A tiny prefab cabin had been set up at the gates near the ruins of the old sentry shelter and the amputated stump of the barrier. Inside: a table, a chair and a small electric heater. On this winter morning, Ossiri was cold. Sitting on the chair, he had his feet propped up on the heater, which was trying with every fibre of its resistors to raise the temperature of the shed by one or two degrees. Hands in his pockets, Ossiri stared intently at this Western Union® poster, which, on behalf of a woman with a seductive smile in Dutch wax print and a boy dressed in fancy, pressured Black immigrants in France to send money back to the "old country".

Send money back to the old country. Something about the hint of self-assurance in her smile, or the tilt of her nose, or the ease with which she posed for the camera, or perhaps just a general overall impression ... But the more he stared at the billboard, the more Ossiri saw a resemblance between his mother and the woman in the photograph. The advertising agency had done an exceptionally brilliant job because to find any similarity between the two women required a feat of hallucination, since, physically, they could not have been more different. What is more, Ossiri's mother never wore Dutch wax print. She wore jeans and simple tops. Always. It was a habit she had adopted in the 1970s when she came back from France after taking her sociology degree. Her personal fashion sense, dubbed that of the emancipated Western woman, earned her a nickname she despised: "the White woman". Though she never hesitated to explain to anyone prepared to listen that so-called African print fabric was a "powerful symbol" of alienation, colonisation and dependence: "The preposterously gaudy culmination of the infernal cycle of humiliations inflicted upon the Negro peoples since slavery." Ossiri had always wondered where they came from, these proclamations and this passion that blazed in his mother's eyes whenever she talked about such subjects.

"With cunning, with irons, with gunpowder, the Whites enslaved our people in their millions, kidnapped them and scattered them on every barren rock and crag along the route to the Americas. Suffering under the lash, the humiliation and the complete negation of their humanity, they were put to work in the plantations just as Farmer Bakary's oxen are put to work ploughing in the muddy field behind his house. Get this into your heads, children: White people are no different from us. They may have problems of scale, but they are just like us. Like us in their flesh and in their souls. Like us in their devotion to the gods. They too make sacrifices so that their fields will be fertile. But whereas we symbolically sacrifice a chicken and let a thin trickle of blood fall upon the soil, uttering a few well-chosen imprecations directed at our ancestors, they feel compelled to spill torrents of blood. Their ancestors viciously tortured and humiliated the son of their God before nailing him to a cross on which he bled to death. To expiate this sin, their God demanded they shed torrents of blood in the propitiatory sacrifices. And so, the White peoples slaughtered millions of Indians so that the soil of the Americas would be fertile. Rivers of the Red Man's blood irrigated the land on which Black slaves would work without respite for four centuries! Get this into your heads, children. During those same four hundred years, the White people of the Americas sold the most financially viable agricultural produce of all time to the rest of the world. The most representative products were sugar cane and cotton. Cotton flooded into Europe. The mills of France, of Britain, of Holland began working at full speed. And the clothing of the White people in those countries improved. Over the years, our enslaved sisters and brothers grew more numerous and more powerful. So powerful that even under the lash, they managed to sing magnificent laments even as they toiled harder. In time, cotton overwhelmed every spinning mill in Europe. However well the White people dressed, however often they changed their clothes and their fashions, they could no longer consume all the cheap cotton coming from Mississippi, Alabama, the Caribbean and the rest of the Americas. It was then that they hit upon a brilliant idea: Africa. Yes, Africa, a vast reservoir of potential customers for cotton fabric, lay untapped a short boat trip away. An Africa where millions of savages still wandered around stark naked. An Africa that the Europeans had carefully carved up into more or less random territories and meticulously shared out between themselves as one might share out the meat of an elephant after a collective hunt. Since the days when they first exchanged mirrors and trinkets for ivory and gold with unwitting tribal chieftains, the White people had fashioned a robust and precise idea of the supposed customs and tastes of the African peoples. In their factories, they transformed skeins of cotton into garishly coloured, deliriously patterned fabrics. The African print was born. The process of transporting millions of Africans several centuries earlier had taught the White people the most efficient ways to stuff the holds of ships with cargo that could struggle and was difficult to load. I need hardly tell you how much easier the task is when the cargo is inert, flexible and folded! Cargo ships were stuffed to the gunnels, sometimes to the upper decks. Miles and miles of fabric were spilled out along our coastline: from Dakar to Nairobi, from Cairo to the Cape. The propaganda of the powerful always finds its echo in the compliance of the weak. African men and African women adopted and adapted this fabric as though it had always existed. African men and African women began to clothe their handsome bodies with this textile of shameful origin and doubtful taste. The preposterously gaudy culmination of the infernal cycle of humiliations inflected upon the Negro peoples since slavery."

Send money back to the old country. Ossiri would never have imagined that a simple poster could transport him so far in space and time. The long evenings of "ex-currics" during which his mother recounted her version of history came back to him in waves, sometimes misting his eyes with a film of lachrymal fluid. People said that Ossiri's mother was very different after her time in France. To her parents' dismay, she turned down the lucrative post offered her by the Ministry for Education as senior lecturer at the University of Abidjan. She had decided to remain the humble secondary school teacher she had been before she left for France to pursue studies that the national university could not offer beyond a certain level. When asked why she made this choice, she baffled her questioners with a Marxist concept known as "the theory of class suicide". She insisted on being heard, and people looked shocked and appalled when she told them that this ideology had been devised and implemented by a man named Amílcar Cabral, a sort of Che Guevara on melanin, a man from Cabo Verde who left to foment revolution in Guinea-Bissau. Whenever Ossiri's mother was short of money, his grandmother spouted harsh words about the "Amil-*caca*-bral", who left his country to poke his nose into things that were none of his business and who was entirely to blame for her daughter refusing to take a post as a great university professor. After committing "class suicide", Ossiri's mother went a step further. Every time she gave birth to a child, she refused to give it a Judaeo-Christian or Muslim name, even if only as a third or fourth name on the birth certificate at the Abidjan registry office. Ossiri, his younger brother Wandji and his little sisters Ohoua and Djèdja had been the only pupils in their classes with African names. As a result, all four ended up in heroic schoolyard fights when taunted by the children randomly called Jean-Claude, Pierre-Émile, Pascal, Jacques-Philippe, Anne-Cécile, Thérèse or Marie-Françoise . . . But somehow it was *their* mother who was called "the White woman". It was ludicrous! When Aké, their father, the great economist, abandoned them to go live with a woman who was less "White", less complicated, less intellectual and more to his taste, "ex-currics" evenings become a sort of family act of solidarity around their mother. Ossiri could still remember words, phrases, whole passages.

"Get this into your heads, children: the *extracurricular subjects* we discuss at home are at least as important as those that you study in class. The school curricula in our country were devised by people who, though doubtless competent, were extremely lazy. They simply adopted the syllabus they inherited from colonial times. Without so much as a thought, they adopted the humiliating, infantilising, racist teachings of colonialism. These days, it is Africans who teach African children to be ashamed of themselves, of their culture, their language, their history, their entire civilisation. These days, African parents teach their own children about the bravery of Vercingetorix, the savagery of the Zulus, the luminous vision of Louis XIV, the blindness of

King Béhanzin, the glories of Napoleon, the spinelessness of Samori Ture, the courage of Henry Stanley, the cowardice of the Makoko people, the benevolence of the Church, the obscurantism of Vodou fetishes... As a way of establishing the supremacy of Judaeo-Christian civilisation over all others, it is much more effective than when it was taught by White colonists. Get this into your heads, children: colonisation's greatest success was education. Therefore, it is only through education, through elementary school education, that we can escape the heavy burden of colonial passivity. At university, it is already too late. By then, young people are already too warped by their fascination with the White man and the 'good Negro' complex. They will do as their masters did. And so, volunteers are needed, men and women who will teach you to learn, to relearn how to be the Africans that we, your parents, would have been had we been taught the value of our own culture, of our ancient civilisation. Get this into your heads, children!"

Together with the music of her words, Ossiri also remembered his mother's slow, poised gestures, those lips that created magnificent biomorphic shapes, the flame that blazed in her eyes, the spellbound expressions of his brother and his sisters... Ossiri remembered everything. And this warmed him much more than the glowing heater beneath his feet.

Send money back to the old country. Part of Ossiri's job was to patrol the skeletal carcasses of the buildings. Broken windows, missing doors, interminable corridors, rooms with no ceilings, courtyards filled with scrap metal, huge metal ramps petrified by rust, obsolete machines of curious forms...Les Grands Moulins de Paris was a magnificent ruin. The glacial winter breezes danced a freezing farandole through this hulking ship washed up on the banks of the Seine. Ossiri liked making his rounds. Aside from the fact that they prevented him from getting a stiff back while spending his nights sitting on an uncomfortable chair in the prefab cabin, often, when he did his rounds, he felt as though he were in one of the Hollywood movies where the lone hero traverses a post-apocalyptic wasteland in search of a redemptive truth hidden somewhere above the chaos. He liked the feeling of vertigo when he looked into a tangle of concrete beams and steel tubes. This is where the grain silos must have been located. By the simple laws of gravity, the wheat cascaded from above, through one machine after another, one sieve after another, and arrived at human level in the form of fine white flour, free of all impurities. Ossiri could not imagine the countless tonnes of grain that had passed through here to create thousands of tonnes of bread that had fed millions of people over many decades. It made his head spin, and he enjoyed this feeling of vertigo.

In the old country, there was a Grands Moulins in Abidjan. It dated back to the time when the country was a colony and had probably been built according to the same principles used by the mills of quai Panhard-et-Levassor. And, since in Côte d'Ivoire, bread was also a staple food, there had been no lack of raw materials to build the silos of Les Grands Moulins d'Abidjan. But despite the combined efforts of the engineers from ORSTOM, the Research Institute for Overseas Development and the INRA, the Institute for Agronomic Research, not a single blade of wheat had ever deigned to grow in the hot, humid tropical climate of Côte d'Ivoire. Ossiri and his siblings had sat for many hours of "ex-currics" on dietary alienation. It was a subject that incensed their mother. At home, there was no bread at breakfast. There never had been. Nor was there milk or butter. Yams, manioc, *riz couché*, bananas in every imaginable form and every possible cooking method: their mother used her fertile imagination so that they never envied classmates who were fed on bread slathered with Président butter, Nestlé sweetened condensed milk or Bonnet Rouge unsweetened condensed milk.

"You need to understand, children, it is impossible to be independent when the food we eat comes from the very people who alienate us. A large percentage of our natural resources is shipped back to the West in exchange for the tonnes of wheat needed to satisfy the whimsical demand for bread. You need to understand, children, bread is a dietary whim, a dietary neurosis, a dietary mimicry, a dietary trauma, a dietary alienation; it is dietary suicide. Call it what you like, but bread is not a staple foodstuff for our people. This is not the Sahara. In Côte d'Ivoire, you can scatter any seeds you like on the ground and, without having to stoop to tend it, within six months you have a baobab! Imagine what we could do with all the money we spend buying wheat from White farmers?"

Truly, Ossiri loved the giddy feeling he got when he stood beneath the silos.

Then he would go around the back of the building, next to the railway tracks. Trains came and went from the gare d'Austerlitz, juddering past with a horrible shriek of metal: the demonic soundtrack for an apocalyptic movie. Usually, it was here that Ossiri stumbled on taggers suffering wall withdrawal. He had never had any problems with them. For street artists, it was all part of the game: when caught, they politely left the premises. But Ossiri always told them that they could come back and finish their piece after his shift; he knew that Kassoum, who did the night shift, never made the rounds. This was probably why there were so many taggers and graffiti artists around. Ossiri would watch, sometimes over a period of several weeks, as veritable frescos blossomed. Visibly, the local street artists had much more to say than the laconic "Fuck The Police!" Ossiri often saw on the walls of estates in the banlieue. After his visit to the "art gallery", he would take his time, slowly making his way around the eastern elevation. All around, the neighbourhood was a forest of cranes, a dance floor for cement mixers. A new neighbourhood was mushrooming on the left bank of the Seine. Office buildings and apartment blocks slowly sprouted from the confusion of the building sites. There was even talk of covering the railway tracks with a huge concrete shell so that the southern facades would be spared the aural and visual pollution of the commuter trains and those heading for the provinces. It was patently obvious that it would not be poor people moving here. Finally, using a shortcut discovered by chance on one of his morning rounds, Ossiri would weave his way through the Moulins via a maze of windswept corridors. End of patrol. Nearby, the prefab cabin. The cabin of the security guard. The cabin of tedium. The cabin with a view of the Western Union® poster.

Send money back to the old country. The decision to come to France was one Ossiri had made. It was not as though he lived in abject poverty in Abidjan. His job teaching natural sciences at a private lycée paid more than enough for him to have a relatively comfortable existence. Young, single, with no children, a mother who housed him for half the year and a decent salary that arrived promptly on the 25th of every month, Ossiri was a well-heeled white-collar worker. He watched as, without a single hiccup, his life unfolded, safely and securely, along well-trodden paths. And it was this that terrified him. A precocious student, he had graduated early. By the age of twenty-three, he had already spent two years teaching. The lesson plans that did not change from year to year; the unvarying wait for his salary to arrive; the wild nights of beer, crude jokes and easy women with colleagues the same age as his mother; the pupils who were sometimes barely younger than he was . . . All these things scared him. Though everyone had told him that things would naturally resolve themselves, it was simply a matter of time. The age difference between him and his pupils could not but increase with the passing years. But he did not feel that he belonged. The wanderlust he felt inside was powerful and utterly unfathomable. Despite all rational discussion and all scientific reasoning, Ossiri wanted to travel. Far. When he talked about going, about leaving everything behind, people called him a madman. In fact, there was even talk of a hex cast on him by the immortals, a powerful spell called "jealous-of-the-success-of-others". Everyone tried to dissuade him. Everyone, except his mother. "Go, see, and come home to us!" she had said. Nothing more. France seemed to him the obvious destination. His mother made no comment. On the day he left, she scribbled a name and number on a scrap of paper. "Ferdinand is a friend. Call him when you arrive. Tell him you are my first-born son. He will help you if you need it."

Send money back to the old country. The winter nights drew in quickly. The billboard was now bathed in the orange glow of the streetlights. The shift he had started twelve hours earlier, at six o'clock in the morning, would soon be over. Usually, these last minutes were the worst, as Ossiri waited impatiently for the night guard to take over. But time passed quickly when he thought back to the traumatic days that had followed his arrival in Paris. During the first four weeks, he had discovered the joys of sleeping on a sofa: going to bed after everyone else, getting up before them. This was in the apartment of an old friend, Thomas, who had been living in France for ten years now. After Thomas's third child was born, social services finally offered him a flat on Les Courtilleraies estate in Le Mée-sur-Seine, some 40 kilometres from Paris, the second-last stop on RER train line D.

The neighbourhood was a constellation of angular, low-rise blocks set amid a tangle of alleys that zigzagged according to some quasi-mystical logic. Clearly, the urban developers who dreamed up the plans for Les Courtilleraies smoked more than tobacco. A thirty-minute walk was enough for Ossiri to realise that Le Mée-sur-Seine was simply a dormitory town. There was nothing to do here other than sleep and go to work, for those who had work. The train to Paris cost as much as a ticket from Abidjan to Ouagadougou and took as long as driving from Abidjan to Assinie.[9] Ossiri's savings quickly depleted. His residence permit expired on the very day he spent his last French francs on a pack of cigarettes. *After this pack of Marlboro Lights, you've got no safety net, buddy*, Ossiri said to himself as he watched the image of Saint-Exupéry on the back of his last fifty-franc note disappear into the till of the bar-tabac. He was now alone on a highwire stretched across the abyss marked deportation.

The notion that a man could be exiled, forcibly removed from home and workplace simply because a police official had failed to sign some routine piece of paper was terrifying. Though Ossiri rather liked the bureaucratic euphemism "escort to the border". It sounded like a bucolic stroll through fields and meadows flanked by a joyful, boisterous entourage to an invisible frontier filled with entrancing mysteries. Once there, the entourage would spontaneously

---

9 Author's note: Assinie is a coastal resort town in south-eastern Côte d'Ivoire, nestled between the river, the sea and the lagoon. Jean-Marie Poiré shot *French Fried Vacation* here.

burst into an acapella rendition of "Auld Lang Syne" sung in the round. The wanderer – or rather the "escortee" – would carry on alone, wiping away a furtive tear. The reality of Ossiri's situation, however, was the antithesis of the idyllic ramble: he felt as though he were under house arrest in Le Mée-sur-Seine. He could not risk taking the train without paying. Being in possession of a valid ticket was a rule to be scrupulously respected when one feared an "escort to the border". Thomas explained that the STIF[10] had fashioned the Paris regional railway network into a vast spider's web designed to catch undocumented immigrants. For most, the prelude to an "escort to the border" began when they attempted to travel under their own steam, perhaps to work or to visit friends or family ... without being in possession of a valid ticket.

When Thomas and his wife were at work, Ossiri went for longs walks around Le Mée-sur-Seine. Looking at the modern buildings, it occurred to him that, had it been in Africa, this town would have been a gated ghetto for the super-rich. Here, it was a sink estate for the unemployed, those on minimum wage and people on welfare. It was a "non-town", an administrative "locality" on a map, a de-marcated zone in a vast, protean urban jungle of which Paris was the centre. To Ossiri, it had something of the air of a concentration camp. He was constantly bumping into the same people, or rather, the same type of people. In this

---

10 Author's note: Syndicat des transports d'Île–de-France.

"non-district" of this "non-town", his "fellow inmates" were fairly evenly divided between Blacks, Arabs and Whites. These were the people exploited by a system that kept them just about alive enough so they could work and consume without complaint. Everyone in this town circled between two nerve centres: the RER train station and the café-cum-bar-cum-tobacconist-cum-betting office. Ossiri could not abide these dreary streets, even when he had something to occupy his time. He preferred to lose himself in his thoughts, smoking cigarettes on the narrow, rickety pedestrian bridge over the railway tracks. He would often stop in the centre while, just under his feet, massive Class BB electric locomotives flashed past, creating a deafening roar and a minor earthquake, hauling dozens of carriages or cargo trucks. These mini-tremors, together with the showers of sparks caused by pantographs brushing against high-voltage cables, represented Ossiri's mental landscape, a sort of magical world that literally held him spellbound. Trains disappeared along a sweeping bend heading for Paris or behind a bank of dilapidated warehouses in the direction of Melun. Ossiri would sometimes stand on the bridge for hours at a time, occupied by various fluttering concerns about his future as an "undocumented immigrant" in France. One day, while watching the 4.42 p.m. Auxerre–Paris roar past, he remembered that the scrap of paper on which his mother had scrawled was still tucked into his wallet. He decided to call Ferdinand.

The journey to Chaville was one of the most stressful he had ever experienced. Since he had no money to pay for a ticket, Ossiri simply jumped the turnstile. "Pub-lic trans-port!" as they say in Abidjan. Every time the train jolted, or indeed any time someone came into the carriage where he was sitting with his buttocks tightly clenched, Ossiri pictured a phalanx of ticket inspectors about to sweep him up and hand him over to specialist officers who dealt with "escorts to the border". Ossiri was no longer convinced that such journeys corresponded with the bucolic idyll to the strains of massed choirs in his imagination. When the sign marked "CHAVILLE" hove into view, he felt a surge of relief. On the phone, Ferdinand had said he would be waiting on the station platform. Ossiri had little trouble recognising him. Ferdinand was the only Black man on the platform, which, for someone coming from Le Mée-sur-Seine, was a conspicuous detail. Ferdinand was a short, beaming man. Apart from his big nose, everything about him radiated discretion. They climbed into a battered old Peugeot 205, red as a glass of Bordeaux on wheels. The car had a strong, unpleasant smell of wet dog. Thankfully, in less than five minutes, they pulled up outside a beautiful, detached house in the middle of a steeply sloping street. Ferdinand's wife, Odette, was also short and beaming. The three of them ate in front of a large television. Endive salad with bacon followed by blanquette of veal and then a Camembert that smelled foul but tasted absolutely delicious. There was even a dessert of poached pears smothered in dark chocolate. It was the first entirely French lunch Ossiri had had since he arrived.

Ferdinand talked nostalgically about Ossiri's mother.

Timidly, but with a certain self-assurance, he talked about the twenty-five years he had spent in France. When he first arrived – thanks to "Uncle" André – he had been employed as a security guard at Les Grands Moulins. He had always been a "serious worker", and he had been "greatly valued" by his bosses. After fifteen years of loyal and faithful service, he had been encouraged to set up his own security company. He sub-contracted the jobs offered to him by his former employers, who, in turn, sub-contracted those assigned to them by larger companies.

"I am the little boss at the end of the chain, boy. I'm the guy who recruits the guards, organises the rotas, pays the staff, takes the risks – in a nutshell, I'm the one who does all the work. But it doesn't bother me, as long as there's something in it for me and for everyone else. I'm always fair and honest with the guards I hire; I always pay them on time, even though I know they're undocumented immigrants. You can't say that about a lot of Ivoirians who run security companies. You'll find that out for yourself. And, actually, I always pay cash, because if I paid by cheque or by bank transfer, they would get ripped off. The so-called brothers or friends whose ID cards they borrow and whose bank accounts they use are never in any hurry to hand over the fruits of their 'labour'. Everyone knows I employ undocumented workers, from the firms who sub-contract me to the préfecture de Police, but they all turn a blind eye, because it suits them. That said, I cover myself as best I can. I insist on a photocopy of a valid residence permit – I don't give a damn where they got it. I'm half-blind these days, so I can always say I can't tell whether they look like the ID photo."

Ferdinand burst into a giggle that was innocent and childlike, in stark contrast to the seriousness of what he had just said. Then, in a somewhat less cynical tone, he said: "I can give you a job; I just hope you're a hard worker like your mother…" Ossiri did not hear another word of Ferdinand's speech. The word "job" set off fireworks in his head at the prospect of financial independence, of a revolution that would bring the tedium of Le Mée-sur-Seine to a swift and bloody end. His thoughts were elsewhere; his ears were deaf. Though Ferdinand reeled off countless comical stories of his time in Paris, Ossiri heard nothing. He had already travelled in time to the first thing he would buy with his first pay packet. It brought back memories of the moment when he first qualified for public service back in Côte d'Ivoire. To keep the conversation going, Ossiri switched to autopilot, placing a well-timed nod to signal his approval, or a "really?" that triggered another anecdote, and most of all, whenever he laughed, he slapped his thighs to keep himself awake. Because, besides being preoccupied by the prospect of work, Ossiri was also exhausted. As someone who had spent most of his life eating nothing but manioc, plantains and yams, the blanquette of veal was proving difficult to digest. His liver was marshalling all its energy and all its digestive juices to deal with the rich sauce of flour, butter and cream that had covered the large morsels of veal. Ossiri half-dozed, his head jolting upright each time he began to nod off. Odette had long since disappeared into the kitchen, from which emerged the warlike clash of cutlery against the raging dishwater. One might think it was extremely rude of Ossiri to doze off during such an intimate conversation. But was Ferdinand truly addressing him? He was talking to himself. He was harking back to the best moments of his life, retracing the long road he had travelled from the village. Hazily and haphazardly, Ossiri heard details of the famous '70s oil crisis, of Les Grands Moulins, of a messiah – who could be male or female, he was not sure – and of many things that made no real sense to him. At the end of the day, when Ferdinand finally fell silent, he handed Ossiri three hundred-franc notes: "Just to tide you over in the meantime . . ." he said. A king's ransom.

"Where are you living?"

"Le Mée-sur-Seine."

"That's near Melun, isn't it?"

"The station just before Melun."

"That's a long way, boy."

". . ."

So, Ferdinand picked up the receiver of a red rotary phone bearing the logo "france télécom". He talked to a man named Jean-Marie about Ossiri's mother. At the end of the call, he said paternally: "You can't stay out there in the suburbs, boy. And I can't put you up here. You need to make your own way in life. Jean-Marie has a room for you at the RSCI. He won't charge you much rent. He knew your mother well. They did a lot of campaigning together back in the day. You start your new job at six o'clock tomorrow morning. It's in central Paris. Tolbiac métro station, quai

Panhard-et-Levassor. A building called Les Grands Moulins de Paris – you can't miss it."

Send money back to the old country. The pretentiously named "outer perimeter" of the site was made up of sheets of corrugated iron, alternately painted fluorescent green and cement grey. A large, rickety metal gate, which creaked as it opened and closed, served as the main entrance. Ossiri opened it to let in the next shift and sometimes for the huge trucks that came to clear the former flour mills of its steel and concrete skeletons. But at this hour, when operated from outside by a Black man dressed in black, it opened in a screech of metal to admit a Peugeot 205, the wine glass on wheels. Ossiri's replacement. Ferdinand's beat-up old jalopy was the company's "command car". Sometimes, Ferdinand would personally drop guards to the sites where they were working. Tonight, it was Kassoum and Joseph. Over the eleven months Ossiri had been working here, the changing of the guard had become as perfectly choreographed as the one at Windsor Castle, the Queen of England's humble country house. The car would pull up in front of the prefab cabin. Ossiri would go out, shake hands with Ferdinand and give him a verbal report that had never yet exceeded three letters: A-OK. Then, he would open the back door and let out an excitable Joseph. Ferdinand would immediately set off, having other security guards to collect. His security company was groaning under the weight of sub-contracted contracts. Then Kassoum would peremptorily close the gate. The Peugeot 205 would speed down the quai Panhard-et-Levassor "four-lane", belching a cloud of black smoke over the Western Union® billboard. "Unclench your arse. Joseph's not going to bite you." Kassoum would always make the same quip as he took the dog's leash from Ossiri. It was certainly true that Ossiri did not feel at ease with the gargantuan beast. The Beauceron's head almost came up to his chest and, despite the sturdy muzzle, Ossiri felt he could not trust a dog whose master had named him Joseph in honour of Stalin, Mobutu and Kabila, three dictators who shared both a first name and a singular sense of cruelty.

Ossiri always left soon after Ferdinand drove off. Kassoum would hole up in the cabin with the portable TV he always brought with him. From that point, he would emerge only to put more kibble in Joseph's bowl whenever he barked too loudly. Beauce Sheepdog was the other name for the breed. Beauce, the French region that produced the tonnes of wheat that had once fuelled the huge silos that had since fallen silent. At night, the ruins of Les Grands Moulins de Paris became the kingdom of Joseph, the Beauce Sheepdog. It was an irony that made Ossiri smile. He walked past the Western Union® billboard, heading towards the Tolbiac Bridge. He walked slowly, despite the bitter cold. He was in no hurry to get back to the RSCI. Since moving from Le Mée-sur-Seine, he had been living at the filthy shithole on the boulevard Vincent-Auriol in the centre of Paris. The RSCI had not been a student residence for many years. In fact, it was no longer a residence at all.

BREAK

LOW MARBLE WALL

The perfect spot for a break. Set opposite the entrance to a large shopping mall, it separates the broad pavement of the Champs-Élysées from the slip road leading down to "Vinci" underground car park. The security guard straddles the low wall and observes the parade of biped fauna on one side and of quadricycle vehicles on the other. During his break, the watchman watches the watchers.

PARADE

During a one-hour break, the following descended into "Vinci" underground car park: one Maserati, two Porches, one large Mercedes-AMG G 63, one red Ferrari, one yellow Ferrari and three BMW X6s. Enough to build a fully equipped regional hospital in Gagnoa, pay the staff and offer free medical treatments for a year. And that is without counting the Peugeots, Renaults, Volkswagens, Audis, Fords and other classic town cars.

FAST ATM

Seven seconds, including the time needed to enter the PIN, this is how long it takes the HSBC ATM on the Champs-Élysées to spit out twenty euros. It takes forty-three seconds for the Crédit Lyonnais on the rue Louis-Bonnet in Belleville to perform the same task! On the Champs-Élysées, money is quickly dispensed, and just as quickly expensed... In poor neighbourhoods, even the cash machines are reluctant to hand over cash.

ROSE OF KASHMIR

In front of the shopping mall, a pot-bellied old man in traditional Hindu dress stands ramrod straight, holding a sign: "*Rose of Kashmir, Indian and Pakistani dishes.*" In Paris, the Kashmiri struggle for independence has been transformed into a rose simply by putting India and Pakistan on the same plate. Mahatma Gandhi would have loved the Champs-Élysées.

RESTLESS STUMP

A homeless Romani beggar sits on the ground and displays the stump of his left leg. He is very excitable; he fidgets and squirms restlessly while muttering to himself in some strange, incomprehensible language. He hurls insults and gibberish at any other Roma who dare invade the imaginary space whose borders he alone can see.

FISHER OF BUTTS

On the kerb of the Champs-Élysées, a man sits on a stool. A mongrel dog dozes next to him. With the serene expression of a Sunday angler, he calmly extends his long fishing rod. A little bucket dangles from the line, and, in it, the growing pile of cigarettes given to him by passers-by.

So successful is our fisherman that he has to empty his little bucket every fifteen minutes. If he smokes them all, he might not survive the winter. If he sells them all, he might spend the winter in Bermuda.

BREAK

In the lingo of security guards, to "take a break" means to stand in for a colleague at another shop while *he* takes a break. In this way, he not only does a favour for his colleague, but he also notches up another hour's overtime. It is also a way of discovering other shops.

BREAK AT THE CHAMPS-ÉLYSÉES BRANCH OF ZARA

At Zara, men's clothing is in the basement, women's clothing is on the ground floor and the first floor is reserved for children's clothing. Woman comes above man and the child comes above everyone.

BREAK AT LA DÉFENSE

At the Sephora outlet in La Défense, the head of security is an Ivoirian of a certain age who goes by the nickname Éric-coco. He is completely possessed by the spirit of Chanel.

Éric-coco, sounding frantic: "While I'm at the back, you keep an eye on the Chanel, especially the 6.8-ounce 5s."

Security guard: "What?"

Éric-coco: "People tend to steal the large No. 5. Oh, and the 3.4-ounce Allure. I need you to stop them."

Security guard: "Okay, but what exactly are we talking about?"

Éric-coco, planting the security guard next to the Chanel stand: "We're talking about Chanel, for god's sake! Chanel No. 5 and Allure de Chanel. Perfume. Premium perfume. Why do you think you're here? To stop people stealing €10 mascaras or €30 bottles of Cacharel? Just stand here and don't move. If you lose a single one, you'll never work in my store again."

BREAK IN LAVALLOIS-PERRET

In this Paris suburb with bourgeois delusions, the Sephora outlet is in the paved, pedestrianised town centre, next to all the other brands that exude fake luxury and fake sophistication. The boutique is not very big, and all the departments are within retina range of the security guard, who does not even need to turn his head. Inside, the atmosphere is muted: staff and customers whisper, perhaps to avoid disturbing the sacred perfumes, perhaps to avoid altering their chemical composition with raised voices. In an outlet of this kind, shoplifting is rare, and the superhuman feat required of the security guard is to avoid falling asleep on his feet.

BREAK IN VINCENNES

The shop in Vincennes stands right outside the castle. Back in the days when it was inhabited by a Louis Umpteenth, body care and bathing were vanishingly rare. They would have been grateful for a branch of Sephora.

FROZEN CULTURE

On the Champs-Élysées, the Virgin Megastore is directly above a branch of Monoprix. The ceiling of the frozen foods section is the floor of the book department. Queen's Ocean Flash-Frozen Alaskan Cod Fillets are just below the new novel by Anna Gavalda: the bland leading the bland.

POLICE PRESENCE

The avenue des Champs-Élysées is teeming with plain-clothes police officers. They always wear a jacket, regardless of the season, and white earbuds plugged into iPhones on which – oh, the wonders of technology! – they live-stream the mugshots of France's Most Wanted. They are easily identifiable at five hundred paces but believe they are utterly invisible. As we say back in Assinie: "Everyone can see a swimmer's back, except the swimmer."

BASTILLE DAY

Armed soldiers march in lockstep down the avenue. At the far end, on the flat pack stands lining the place de la Concorde, sit all the political reprobates the Fifth Republic has to offer. It would not even occur to these heavily armed knuckleheads to make a clean sweep. Yet there is a precedent: Anwar Sadat. Egypt, 1981. Using parade rifles loaded with live ammunition, a handful of soldiers relieved the Egyptian people of their leaders during a similar parade. Sadat and a number of his ministers died in the attack. They were quickly replaced by Mubarak and his clique. These days, seeing the protests on Tahrir Square and the procession of dead civilians that inevitably follows, it seems as though the Egyptians have chosen a more masochistic approach to political opposition and the change of power.

BASTILLE DAY 2

The obelisk on the place de la Concorde is the hard cock, the Arc de Triomphe is the arsehole and the Champs-Élysées is the erogenous perineal zone that connects the two. With all these ramrod soldiers and titillated politicians, it is safe to say that today is the day the Republic tosses itself off.

BASTILLE DAY 3

The most surprising thing is not the parade of all this lethal weaponry. The surprising thing is the public cheering and applauding.

SUPER SECURITY GUARD

Boredom, feelings of futility and waste, lack of creative outlet, exaggerated aggression response, lack of imagination, infantilisation, etc., are the corollaries of a career as a security guard. And yet, a soldier is merely an overblown form of security guard.

SECURITY TRAINING

In order to practise his profession, a security guard must have a permit from the préfecture de Police. And these days, the security guard must complete mandatory security training. A diploma that earns him the right to stand for twelve hours for minimum wage in a branch of Franprix or a skeezy suburban branch of Ed where his mission is to stop kids from pilfering cans of Coke ... In reality, the aforementioned training consists of memorising Articles 53–73 of the Code of Criminal Procedure. As with all judicial texts, a series of convoluted and grandiloquent sentences is used to communicate something extremely simple. Articles 53–73 deal with the concept of *in flagrante delicto* and broadly state that anyone who catches a person in the act of stealing has the right to treat the person as a thief and pursue them. Yes, my fellow citizens, in the eyes of the law, we are all security guards.

RETURN TO SEPHORA, CHAMPS-ÉLYSÉES

REBEL, REBEL

A woman in a burqa is carrying a little basket in which there is a bottle of *Lady Rebel* by Mango.

REVOLUTIONARIES

So pleased were young Tunisians by the "Jasmine Revolution" they had launched in their own country, which resulted in the overthrow of the dictator Ben Ali, that battalions of them took the Mediterranean by storm and found themselves in France. With little education, a limited grasp of the language of Jamel Debbouze, and left to their own devices, they spend their days in Paris much as they did in the ghettos of Sousse or Tunis: between idleness and petty theft. For them, the height of elegance and fashion is to dress like the young people from the French banlieues. But they have neither the swagger nor the lingo that go with it and, as a result, are easily recognisable.

Security guards have dubbed them the "revolutionaries". Which sometimes leads to comical exchanges over their headsets.

"Heads up, three revolutionaries prowling around the Good Dye Young stand!"

"Revolutionary uprising in Bath & Body."

"Man the barricades, the revolutionary in the red baseball cap has a Sauvage body spray in his underpants."

ONLY THE BRAVE

A "revolutionary" has been seen in the act of shoplifting. Until he leaves the shop, he cannot be searched or considered a thief. But, if he jettisons the fragrances whose packaging he has disembowelled, he must pay for them. There follows a surreal low-speed chase in which security guard and shoplifter calmly wander around the shop side by side. After almost half an hour of this preposterous game, the "revolutionary" cracks and loudly and intelligibly demands his own arrest. Down his trousers, two bottles shaped like clenched fists: *Diesel*, Only the Brave.

DIALOGUE

A smug man speaking to a security guard: "That black suit makes you look like Samuel L Jackson in *Jackie Brown*."

Security guard: "I think you mean *Pulp Fiction*."

Smug man: "What?"

Security guard: "*Pulp Fiction*."

Smug man: "No, *Jackie Brown*, the one with the sexy Black chick in it."

Security guard: "Samuel L Jackson doesn't wear a black suit in that movie, Monsieur. He has a dayglo-green jacket and wears his Kangol cap backwards. Whereas in *Pulp Fiction ...*"

Smug man: "Really? You know a lot about film, do you?"

The man looks at him doubtfully and carries on walking down the aisle.

LEOPARD PRINT

Handbags, slacks, scarves, chadors, shoes, dresses, etc., leopard print seems to be in fashion for a great number of women. Millions of years of evolution went into creating the perfect camouflage for the jungle, one that is now used to attract as much attention as possible in the city.

> *O, Leopard, peerless hunter, noble feline,*
> *robed in thy subtle camouflage and stealing*

> *through deepest forest, hidden from your prey*
> *know that there are women of today*
> *who wear your pelt and think themselves your peer*
> *but hunt for men amid the urban drear.*

RELATIVE COCCYX DISTANCE THEORY

There is a theory that links the position of the coccyx relative to the seat of a chair to the level of remuneration.

The theory may be stated thus: "In any profession, the greater the distance between coccyx and seat, the lesser the corresponding salary." In other words: salary is inversely proportional to time spent in a standing position. The security guard's payslip is proof of this theory.

LILIANE AND BERNARD

Liliane Bettencourt is the principal shareholder in L'Oréal, which accounts for 80 per cent of the perfume and cosmetics brands sold at Sephora.

Bernard Arnault is the principal shareholder of the LVMH group, which owns the Sephora brand.

Like a couple of old-fashioned apothecaries, Liliane brews up potions in the back kitchen for Bernard to sell in the shop.

A REASSURING THOUGHT

Albeit to an infinitesimal degree, the work of the security guard contributes to the wealth of Bernard and Liliane.

A DISCOURAGING THOUGHT

Without the security guard's labours, the wealth of Bernard and Liliane would not be affected, even to the most infinitesimal degree.

PFF!

Do humans heave a loud sigh, puff out their cheeks and scowl because they are exasperated? Or to let others know they are exasperated? Or both? Whatever the case, *Pff!* is commonly articulated by certain men as they hesitate in the doorway before following their wives into the shop.

SENSE(S)

In the perfume aisles, soft lighting is used to heighten the sense of smell.

In the make-up aisles, harsh lighting is used to heighten the sense of vision.

Everywhere, mediocre muzak is used to heighten the sense of deafness.

DEGRESSIVE RANGE

On a sliding scale, the five senses have a decreasing range: Sight, Hearing, Smell, Touch, Taste.

AGGRESSIVE RANGE

Sometimes, the children of Gulf Arabs who run amok in the boutique remind the security guard of Abdullah, the irritating little brat, son of the Emir Mohammed Ben Kalish Ezab in *Tintin: Land of Black Gold*.

THE SECURITY GUARD AND THE PRINCESS

When the elegant Arabic woman of about fifty, dressed in Western clothes, steps into the shop, a buzz quickly ripples through the sales staff. Everyone recognises her. For his part, the security guard notices nothing beyond the fact that the woman is flanked by two of the beefiest bodyguards ever encountered north of the 33rd parallel. So, when the woman comes over, looks at him and speaks in Arabic, the security guard rouses himself from his inner life to evaluate the threat posed by the two giant hominids standing behind her. With a single blow, either of these men could snuff out a life, inner or otherwise.

The woman: "ميس باش هنا"

Megasapiens 1: "Her Highness says that you are a very handsome young man."

Security guard: "..."

The woman: "ودبي نمك تنك أعرف ذنم فرتق ط طوليه"

Megasapiens 1: "Her Highness says that you remind her of someone that she knew long ago."

Security guard: "..."

The woman: "خصوصا عم القليل هل سكوكة"

Megasapiens 1, smiling: "Especially with that little goatee beard."

Security guard, stroking his goatee: "..."

The woman: "وهنبو كانآبآء الذين شاعوا فى المملكة علاعربية السعودية"

Megasapiens 1: "Her Highness asks whether you have any relatives who lived in Saudi Arabia."

Security guard: "Please tell Her Highness that the only dunes my family have ever known are the sand dunes on Vridi beach in Abidjan, in the Côte d'Ivoire."

Megasapiens 1 to the woman: "ولادهيد علع لا امرلا نم الشاطي. اهنا تأتي من حاسل اعلاج. نعرف أن"

The woman's lips curl into a magnificent smile that reveals her impeccable teeth.

Megasapiens 1: "Her Highness says that you are as funny as the man she once knew."

The woman: "أشكركم علع ذخأ الوقت لتحدث معي"

Megasapiens 1: "Her Highness thanks you for taking the time to speak with her."

And the woman disappears into the boutique without a second glance at the security guard. The two brick shithouses follow.

THE PRIME MINISTER, THE PRESIDENT'S SON
AND THE MONEY OF THE HOUSE OF SAUD

Over the security guards' headsets:

Cheick, a Senegalese guard: "Next to the Givenchy stand, that's Ousmane Tanor Dieng, the ex-prime minister of Senegal."

Sam, a Congolese guard: "Do you think he'll steal the perfume?"

Djab, an Ivoirian guard: "Ha, ha, ha! We'll be all over him like a cheap suit."

Kaket, a Cameroonian guard: "What about the presumption of innocence?"

Cheick: "He's not going to steal anything. He's already stolen more than enough to buy up the whole shop if he wants to."

Djab: "In that case, he's a repeat offender. We need to stick to him like leeches."

Cheick: "Rumour has it that, a few years ago, the President's son went to Saudi Arabia to visit the Royal Family, where he was given a huge sum in cash for some reason or other. Instead of taking a direct flight back to Senegal, he went via France. At the airport, overzealous customs officers found a suitcase full of cash and arrested the

President's son. His father quickly intervened and, to avoid a diplomatic incident, the customs officers released the son but kept the suitcase. Since his son had no official role, the President sent the Prime Minister on a diplomatic visit to France so that he could retrieve the money. Apparently, when he came back to Senegal, the Prime Minister told the President that the suitcase had been lost. Pure and simple. Since the money did not officially exist, the President could not demand an explanation for fear of that news of the affair might leak. Apparently, it was a couple of hundred thousand West African CFA francs."

Kaket: "What about the presumption of innocence?"

Sam: "Oh, shut up, Kaket!"

Djab: "Cheick, get off the line. You're doing our heads in."

Cheick: "OK, OK, OK. J4 in a baseball cap at the make-up stand!"

SECURITY GUARDS IN THE MOVIES

In the tens of thousands of movies and B-movies that have been made since the Lumière brothers first made *The Arrival of a Train at La Ciotat*, no security guard has ever been a hero. On the contrary, security guards are usually the characters who are quickly and casually killed off as part of the hero's plan to get to the final confrontation with the bad guy in the last scene.

The last scene of Brian De Palma's *Scarface*, when Tony

Montana's house is attacked, is a perfect example of the senseless slaughter of security guards in cinema.

MITSUBISHI

At the entrance to the store, fixed to the wall above the security gate, and therefore directly in the security guard's line of sight, are four large TV screens. In an endless loop, they quadruply show adverts for perfumes by Giorgio Armani and Dior.

- *Armani Adverts*: Shot in HD video, impressionistic storyboarding with lots of strobing effects, tight close-ups, chiaroscuro, artificial settings, high-definition slo-mo shots, sculpted abs, bee-stung lips, moody looks, sensuous hands, lingering final kiss, 23 seconds and precisely 18 shots.
- *Dior Adverts*: Shot on celluloid, film grain visible, classic storyboarding alternating between wide shots and close-ups, bee-stung lips, moody looks, sensuous hands, lingering final kiss, 20 shots in a 23-second spot.

The screens showing the ads are marked with the trefoil logo of Mitsubishi, a company that, long ago, made engines for aircraft and warplanes, including the famous Japanese A6M "Zero" used during the Second World War. So, there was a time when Mitsubishi made devices whose ultimate aim was to prevent the Japanese from being invaded by ads for Dior and Armani.

THE PSG THEORY

In all, or almost all, of the shops in Paris, all, or almost all, of the security guards are Black men. This illuminates on the quasi-mathematical link between three factors: Pigmentation of the skin, Social status and Geography (PSG).

From this, the "relative theory of PSG" can be stated as follows: "In Paris, elevated levels of melanin are correlated to a particular predisposition towards the security professions."

However, all across the world, administrative factors, received ideas, levels of education, racism – whether blatant or latent – economic constraints, etc., routinely stigmatise and pigeonhole people with particularly high pigmentation levels. This may be seen as the "general theory of PSG".

In the West, for example, the higher the level of melanin, the greater the probability that social status will approach zero. With the notable exception of the Romani people. The Roma are White, but their ancestors must have shat upon Marian shrines and papal basilicas from a great height. This alone might explain the curse visited upon their descendants. Hundreds of generations later, Gypsies are the only White people who are more disfavoured than Blacks. On the X-axis, the curve representing their social status remains close to absolute zero.

PIGMENTARY DILUTION

The further one travels from Paris, the more the complexion of security guards tends towards that of butter. In the provinces, in the dark depths of rural France, there are apparently places with White security guards.

AUCTION

All of the sales assistants at Sephora are awarded performance-related bonuses on the products they represent. All of them have developed techniques for luring customers in and persuading them to buy one perfume rather than another. Most simply spray the passing customer with perfume or hand out pre-soaked scent strips while babbling a few words or, at most, a whole sentence.

But one of the male sales assistants has become famous for his technique. Like the newspaper sellers or yesteryear, he loudly vaunts the merits of his fragrances, offering a glimpse of the wonders to be found within. The security guard has nicknamed him the "Town Crier".

THE TOWN CRIER'S TECHNIQUE

Below is the unexpurgated Town Crier's sales spiel for *Narciso Rodriguez*, his new fragrance this week:
"It is forbidden to forbid . . .

"*Narciso Rodriguez*,

"A fragrance that is beguiling, bewitching, bewildering.

"Allow yourself to be beguiled by the sensual notes of musk, bewitched by bright notes of bergamot.

"A breath of amber wreathed in a cloak of castoreum.

"It is forbidden to forbid . . .

"*Narciso Rodriguez*,

"A fragrance that is beguiling, bewitching, bewildering."

. . . repeat ad libitum.

A week ago, he was proclaiming the glories of *Bleu de Chanel* using precisely the same spiel with the exception of the opening line and the name of the product.

"Beneath the paving stones, the beach . . .

"*Bleu de Chanel*,

"A fragrance that is beguiling, bewitching, bewildering.

"Allow yourself to be beguiled by the sensual notes of musk, bewitched by bright notes of bergamot.

"A breath of amber wreathed in a cloak of castoreum.

"Beneath the paving stones, the beach . . .

"*Bleu de Chanel*,

"A fragrance that is beguiling, bewitching, bewildering."

. . . repeat ad libitum

Security Guard: "Don't regulars ever interrogate you?"

The Town Crier: "Of course not. People don't understand this shit, and they don't want to understand it. They just want to buy it. What appeals to them is the melody of the words. That's why I'm particularly proud of 'castoreum'. It sounds just perfect, doesn't it?"

The Town Crier has confided his secrets. Next week,

he will be working the Givenchy concession. His spiel will begin, "Be realistic, demand the impossible..." With his bible of student slogans of '68, in theory he could carry on for months. But the security guard remains sceptical; he cannot believe the Town Crier will extol the virtues of Dior with "Down with the carcass of Stalinism". Or Yves Saint Laurent with "Art is dead, don't eat its corpse". Let alone Kenzo with "The barricade blocks the street but opens the way".

ESPRIT DE CORPS

Still standing, the trait of the security guard.

ESPRIT DE CORPSE

Still standing, the fate of the security guard.

ESCORT GIRLS, TRANS WOMEN AND HIJABIS

At about one o'clock in the morning, the high-class escort girls and trans women who ply their trade on the Champs-Élysées and surrounding areas drop by to freshen their fragrance and touch up their outlandish make-up. They share the aisles with women in hijabs, who, for reasons no-one knows, are numerous at this hour. They can be seen chatting together confidentially. The paucity of customers and the enchantment of the night dissolve all barriers, social, moral and religious. All too soon, the escorts and the trans women will go back to their johns, among them some of the husbands of the women in hijabs with whom they have been exchanging beauty tips.

COSMETIC KLEPTOMANIACS

In the boutique, make-up artists offer a facial depilation service. It is only after the service, when they are leaving, that customers are expected to pay. A number of seemingly respectable old biddies regularly avail themselves of these depilation sessions, then wander the aisles aimlessly until they have been "forgotten" and, in turn, "forget" to pay. These are the cosmetic kleptomaniacs. "I completely forgot" is the excuse they invariably trot out if stopped at the door. It would appear that, for elderly ladies from well-heeled neighbourhoods, eyebrow threading causes temporary amnesia.

THIEF

The floppy, chestnut fringe, the flawless side-parting, the perfectly ironed blue-grey shirt, the immaculate black trousers that fall over neatly polished shoes, all these make him look like a British prime minister on his day off. Yet, there is something incongruous in this portrait of the ideal brother-in-law. It is unusual to have a backpack and a shoulder bag when dressed, as though about to do a PowerPoint presentation to an urban planning consultancy. Indeed, the nonchalant air as he stands next to the Dior concession is a little "hammy". A filmmaker's term. This man is "iffy". A security guard's term. But no-one has seen him do anything suspicious. Confirmation comes over the headset: "*J5 in a tie at the Dior concession – nothing to report.*" The Dior concession is the first the customer encounters when he enters the store or the last as he leaves it. Will the man venture further into the store or leave straight away? Which direction will he take? With his sidelong looks and squints, it is the security guard who now looks "shifty". A thief's term. The man does not move. He enters into conversation with one of the salesgirls working the concession. Given the distance and the trite tunes of the talentless blaring from the speakers, the security guard cannot hear a word of what is being said. The salesgirl smiles. Apparently, the man is pleasant company.

On this early summer evening, the store is thronging with customers, making it impossible to focus on one man. A large group enters. Their accents are Slavic. Poles? Russians? Czechs? Their shoes are covered with a fine but visible layer of white dust. They have clearly been to the Louvre and amassed this layer of dust walking through the Jardin des Tuileries. It is the most direct route from the Louvre to the Champs-Élysées, and most tourists stroll all the way to the Arc de Triomphe. The branch of McDonald's next to Sephora is where they stop off after this marathon. The staff at Mickey D's call them "the palefoot".

A "palefoot" woman approaches the security guard. She is accompanied by a sullen child clutching a balloon shaped like a smiling Mickey Mouse on the end of a plastic stick. She wants to know where to find the métro. The security guard points. The gaping maw of George V métro station is fifty metres up the street: this is the nearest métro station. Glancing over the woman's shoulder, the security guard sees the man with the floppy fringe. He is creeping out of the store, hugging the far wall. Their eyes meet. In both their minds, a penny drops. An invisible and inaudible starting pistol has just been fired. The man with the floppy fringe is quick off the starting blocks, sprinting down the avenue. The security guard is slower to react. The long hours spent standing have left his joints stiff. He gets off to a bad start. Whoever the thief is, he now has a ten-metre head start. He glances over his shoulder and sees the security guard is running after him. There are no shouts, no screams. There will be no hue and cry. This is a game of cat and mouse. The thief is the scurrying mouse. The security guard the predatory cat.

The Champs-Élysées is crowded. The thief zigs, the security guard zags. At the thirty-metre mark, the security guard's biomechanics grind into gear and he begins to close the gap. Glancing over his shoulder again, the thief notices. In a feat of remarkable dexterity, he manages to disentangle the bag slung over his shoulder without breaking his stride and tosses it behind him. Jettisoned ballast or a votive offering or both. But the security guard keeps going. He had anticipated this manoeuvre and hurdles the bag before it even hits the polished granite slabs of the pavement. The thief continues to zig. The security guard to zag. Faster and faster. In this human tsunami, they look like a combine harvester ploughing through a wheat field at harvest. The thief's necktie flutters behind him, hovering parallel to the ground in the headwind. The security guard's tie does likewise. *When two men wearing neckties run in the same direction, their ties point in the opposite direction, tracing parallel lines above the racetrack*: I need to remember this new theorem, thinks the security guard as he puts on a burst of speed and lengthens his stride. A few more metres and the thief will be within his grasp. Just before the rue La-Boétie, that would be perfect. Suddenly, the traffic light ahead turns red, triggering an understandable reaction in the security guard, who is familiar with the highway code: he stops. But this is merely a coincidence. In the mind of the security guard, another red light flashes. One that is even more arresting than the lights at a crossroads. What is he thinking running after this man? What if he's armed and dangerous? What if he's crazy? What if the security guard goes crazy? What great moral imperative is satisfied by pursuing a perfume thief? How absurd is it to hunt down a man who has stolen from Bernard, the richest person in France, a frivolous frippery made by Liliane, the seventh richest? What zeal! What a preposterous lack of objectivity and judgement! This is probably how you contract "floko guard" syndrome. The colonial guard with his white truncheon, his inane grin and his fez . . . red. Red means stop. The thief vanishes into the crowd. The security guard retraces his steps. In the jettisoned shoulder bag, he finds three bottles of perfumes: *Elixir Pour Homme* by Azzaro, Diesel *Fuel for Life*, *Allure* by Dior.

WHEN THE MUSIC STOPS 2

Two o'clock in the morning. The store is closing.

An army of nightshift workers wheels carts filled with merchandise through the aisles, restocking displays stripped bare during the day. COs – cleaning operatives – glide across the floors on curious contraptions that wash the tiles and shampoo the carpets. All the COs are Black (cf. *Relative PSG Theory*). They tidy, organise, polish, clean, dust, shampoo, and wipe down every flat surface larger than 2 cm^2.

The speakers set into the false ceiling are finally liberated from the sounds of David Guetta and the Black Eyed Peas. Amy Winehouse died today.

THE AGE OF LEAD

At first, like most people, Kassoum refused to believe what he was seeing. At first, he assumed that there was a glitch with his little Haier portable TV. Everyone had warned him about Chinese electronics. But the grizzled old Asian guy at Montreiul Flea Market had a whole crate of them and was selling them for a hundred francs apiece. A small, easily portable, colour television that worked on both mains and battery: you couldn't get better value for money. Kassoum had not hesitated for a second. He never suffered buyer's remorse; in fact, he became so fond of his little TV he nicknamed it "Aya"[11]. He had only to flip up the little silver aerial and the picture appeared, as clear and bright as on those big, state-of-the-art TVs made in Europe. True, he had

---

11 Author's note: *Haier*, a Chinese brand of household appliances, and *Aya*, a popular girl's name among the Baoulé people are homophones in French.

never quite managed to tune in France 2, France 3, La 5 or Arte. But that didn't matter since, whenever he did manage to catch a few seconds of snowy images of those channels, they had nothing good to say. They were "big-talk" channels. Especially this Arte shit. The screen was always filled with the taking heads of White people filling your ears with speeches as long as tapeworms. At Le Colosse in Treichville, Kassoum had learned to be wary of "big-talkers". They were the canniest crooks in town. Sit in front of them for five minutes and they could sell you anything, and before you knew it you no longer owned the underpants you had on. On Aya, Kassoum could watch the only two channels that mattered to him: TF1 and M6.

But what was wrong with Aya today? TF1 and M6 were broadcasting exactly the same footage. It was as though buttons "1" and "6" on his universal remote control had been merged into one. Granted, both channels were vying for the maximum number of "eyeballs" to absorb their endless ads breaks, so tended to copy each other. But never, in the history of television, to this degree. Besides, right now there should be a game show on TF1 and an American cop show on M6, or maybe the other way round; Kassoum could not remember now. Maybe it was the shock. Instead, both channels were broadcasting footage of twin towers looking over New York City. One of the giant towers was belching black smoke into the clear blue sky of the Indian summer. And while he flicked between Channel 1 and Channel 6 trying to figure out what was going on, Kassoum wondered whether he had really seen a plane trying to fly straight through the other twin in a fearsome fireball. No, there had to be something wrong with Aya. This couldn't be happening now, live from New York ... No, Aya clearly had a kink in her cathode ray tube ... This couldn't be World War III. It was impossible. White people, as Kassoum knew, always did things by the book. Not like this. Not without debates in congress, roundtables at the UN, press conferences, solemn declarations and a bunch of hoopla to prove they were civilised people before they went out and slaughtered each other like savages. After several minutes of this delusion, a reporter, obviously some bumbling trainee, reported that several planes were flitting around American airspace looking to make landings as ground-breaking as the one Kassoum had just seen on Aya's cyclopean face. On TF1, Jean-Pierre Pernaut suddenly reappeared, although his usual stint as news anchor on the One O'Clock News had ended hours earlier. Finally, a proper journalist. Finally, some proper news. Kassoum could not thank TF1 enough. Finally, he could rid his mind of doubt and confusion. Pernaut was here, unexpectedly late in the afternoon, but he was here. This meant that things were serious. Le Pernaut adopted his gravest and most solemn face. He could not have looked more distraught and disgusted if he had been reporting that a gang of Blacks and Arabs had beaten up a penniless French pensioner and robbed her of her meagre savings. "America is under attack by Arab terrorists. And with it, the whole civilised world is faced with the onslaught of barbaric Arab terrorism ..." Pernaut did not pull his punches. So, it was true. This was happening in the United

141

States of America. Two skinheads and three bald guys armed with Stanley knives had outsmarted the security systems, dribbled past the intelligence services, duped the counterterrorist services, and taken civilian planes filled with humans and high-octane fuel – two particularly volatile elements taken singularly – and transformed them into flying bombs. Now, live on worldwide satellite television, they were vying to see which of them could stage the most innovative and lethal landing. A gang of these pantomime terrorists even managed to fly a Boeing into the Pentagon, the headquarters building of the United States Department of Defense. The Pentagon, one of the most secure buildings in the whole world. Kassoum had seen a documentary on M6 that said that if a bluebottle flew over the Pentagon without a duly completed, certified and signed permit, it would be pulverised by a surgical strike from anti-aircraft missiles. And now, here was some shithead parallel parking a Boeing in the car park of the Pentagon. But for the solemn face of Jean-Pierre Pernaut, Kassoum would have assumed the whole story was a joke in particularly poor taste made by someone with the intelligence of a sea slug. In Togo, the police could have easily uncovered a plot like this without even having to consult a vodounsi[12]. Houphouët-Boigny himself, a past master in uncovering fake plots against his own regime, would have dismissed his advisors as lacking imagination if they had proposed such a scenario.

---

12 Author's note: A Vodou shaman.

And yet, on TF1 and on M6, the twin towers were still smouldering, framed in 16/9 widescreen and broadcast in high definition by CNN, NBC, HBO, ABC, etc. – all the American channels with three-letter acronyms. Just as a crowd always gathered at a road accident, so Kassoum and the rest of the planet had been turned into obscene televisual voyeurs, feeding on the misfortune of others. Wide-angle shot: an unrealistic image of two smoking towers in the midst of the downtown Manhattan skyscrapers. Mid-shot: whorls of black smoke licking the facades of the burning buildings. Close-up: flames spreading from floor to floor above the gaping holes made by the Boeing jets, someone at the window waving a white curtain to call for help, men in suits and ties leaping into the void still clutching their briefcases . . . Unspeakable horror in every frame. Then the TV pundits letting themselves get carried away in extended circumlocutions filled with qualifiers. It was the kind of commentary you might hear when a player like Ronaldo, Pibe de Oro, Romário, Butragueño or Rivaldo dribbled a ball into the penalty area. Reality TV. Brutality TV. CEOs and cleaning ladies, securities traders and security guards, bored dispatch riders and board directors, people who, only minutes earlier, had nothing in common, now shared the same tragic fate in these twin prisons of fire, steel and concrete.

In his preposterous prefab, Kassoum could not sit still, a pitiful watchman amid the crumbling skeletal buildings of Les Grands Moulins de Paris. To add to the gloom, Joseph began to bark, to howl at the moon. With everything that

143

was going on, Kassoum had forgotten to refill Joseph's dog bowl. To silence the Beauceron, he raced outside with a double helping, dashing across the courtyard to the makeshift kennel he had fashioned under a huge window. Kassoum filled the huge hound's bowl to the brim then sprinted back to regain his televisual trance. But when he collapsed in front of Aya's eye again, something had changed. A vast cloud of smoke and dust now covered every camera lens. Aya had been blinded by particularly high concentration of ash particles moving towards the cameras faster than the shockwave from an explosion produced by several tonnes of TNT. From a dramatic but relatively low-key documentary, it had become a summer blockbuster, the tentpole Hollywood blockbuster. Except that in this case, Bruce Willis had gone into hiding, Will Smith had disappeared, Arnold Schwarzenegger was suffering from myasthenia gravis. As people watched helplessly, the South Tower of the World Trade Center was collapsing, its spindly legs trembling, its belly filled with the thousands of men and women who had gone there to make their fortune. No sooner had the dust settled than the North Tower began to fall with an indescribable boom that was drowned out by the voice of woman hysterically shrieking "Oh My God" too close to the main camera, which was focused on the upper floors of the North Tower, what in the business is called a "money shot". This cameraman did not allow himself to be affected by the collective hysteria generated by this incomprehensible spectacle. He remained stoic. He did not tremble, unlike the other cameramen who panned down, attempting to follow the giant's fall, their lenses quavering and twirling as they fled this event for which no human being, even an American, was prepared. No, this particular cameraman was from another planet. This cameraman did not blink; his focus did not shift. So, the tower gradually dropped out of the frame, gradually disappearing in the huge billows of dust created as, one after another, floors were crushed to powder. Off screen. Majestic. And the second tower vanished.

Ironically, the last thing viewers saw of the tower was the television aerial proudly mounted on the roof. Kassoum did not know what to think. Pernaut and his fellow presenters took over. 3,000, 6,000, 10,000 . . . so began the mournful litany of the number of dead who might be buried beneath the rubble of the collapsed towers. Experts rushed to offer informed opinions on the sets hastily improvised for the occasion. Reality had already exceeded even their wildest predictions. But they did not have the humility to accept it. They continued to spout their lunatic ravings. Kassoum spent so long listening to these baleful experts that he jumped in fright at the metallic creak of the main gate sliding open: the relief had arrived to take over. Ossiri appeared, wearing a blue jacket, black trousers and black shoes. Like an overexcited child, Kassoum rushed out to meet him.

"After today, the world will never be the same again. Take my word for it: a month from now, you and I won't have a job.

Or at least, not with Uncle Ferdinand." This was how Ossiri concluded his argument. Kassoum had allowed himself to be swept along by Ossiri's calm, authoritative voice, his confident gestures, his profound insight. He had listened with almost religious reverence. How could he be so lucid, so clear-sighted at such a moment? Kassoum had always been fascinated by Ossiri. On the first day, Ossiri arrived at the RSCI, it had been Jean-Marie – the godfather of room allocations – who had personally insisted he move into room 612, where three residents were already in a space of less than 100 square feet. Ossiri had a lost look about him, and it was clear from his eyes that he was wondering where he had washed up. What was this strange place in the middle of Paris? What nightmare was he floating in?

Kassoum had seen the same expression on many new-comers when they first encountered the RSCI. Especially those who came straight from the airport. When they flew from Abidjan to Paris, they assumed they were leaving hell for heaven. This was the mindset of everyone in Abidjan, whether or not they had ever considered emigrating. After all the sacrifices they had made, all the money distributed to the "*canonniers*" who specialised in producing genuine fake papers, after the long, humiliating hours queuing at the French Consulate, after the party thrown to celebrate getting a precious Schengen visa, after the ceremonial farewells and the endless blessings... finally, they had arrived in El Dorado – how could they have ended up in this filthy, ramshackle, tumbledown overcrowded hell-hole in the heart of the French capital; how could such a stinking cesspit exist in the midst of "paradise"? A former resident of the RSCI had managed to bring his 13-year-old daughter from the country. He moved her into the "RCSI suite" he shared with his mistress, their two young children and the dog that came with his job. The "RCSI suites" were the largest rooms in the RSCI, almost 180 square feet with fitted kitchen and en-suite bathroom. By carefully arranging a few inexpensive plywood panels, they could be subdivided into separate areas to create the illusion of a living room and one or even two bedrooms: the lap of luxury. After the initial joy and excitement of seeing her father again, the little girl from Abidjan could not help but ask when they could go to his house, his *real* house, in Paris. The story did the rounds of the residence, and many residents laughed so hard they got a stitch in their sides.

Kassoum had never looked like a newcomer. Having spent eleven years living in Le Colosse, one of the worst of the Treichville ghettos, anywhere else was luxurious. Le Colosse was a tangle of small wooden shacks crowded between the roadbed of the railway tracks and the pillars of the old Houphouët-Boigny Bridge that spanned the inlet of the lagoon separating Treichville from the Plateau.[13] It was a split-level bridge, with a motorway for cars set

---

13 Author's note: The administrative centre and business district. Whether in Dakar, in Brazzaville or in Abidjan, the government district of most colonial capitals was located "on the Plateau", an area of high ground intended to signal its importance, or so they could see trouble coming!

above the long reinforced-concrete tunnel used by the train – the only train in the country, which alternated every twenty-four hours between Abidjan and Bobo-Dioulasso in neighbouring Burkina Faso. Le Colosse began as a series of makeshift huts hidden between the footings of the bridge, then gradually the train tunnel itself was populated by the desperate, the dispossessed, the homeless, those of no fixed abode, the bootblacks, the stallholders and the street hawkers, but also the thieves, the petty gangsters, the pick-pockets, the pimps and the two-bit whores, all those who had never had a taste of the bounteous manna and fell from the Ivoirian cocoa plantations. And so, unseen, one of the most terrible ghettos was born, one of the most feared neighbourhoods in the city. The bridge and tunnel afforded protection from the elements, so for those living in Le Colosse, where and how they would sleep was the least of their worries. Every day, they simply had to find enough to eat. Sleep was a terrible thing for those tormented by hunger. "He who sleeps forgets his hunger." Whoever came up with this nonsensical proverb had never been kept awake by the shrieks and spasms of twenty-six feet of intestine filled with nothing but air. They had never woken in the middle of the night to the seething siren of a brain in thrall to an empty belly, commanding the body to find something to eat by any means necessary. At Le Colosse, it did not matter where you slept. What mattered was what you did in the city before slinking back to the shelter of the ghetto.

Kassoum arrived at the RSCI without even enough

luggage to fill the Leader Price plastic bag loaned to him by his cousin. Although there were already three mattresses on the floor, to Kassoum, Room 612 was like a palace. So enthusiastic and so happy was he at the RSCI that he was quickly adopted by his roommates and by some of the residence's elders. Kassoum addressed everyone as *vieux père* – old father – a mark of respect to which Ivorians were particularly sensitive. Living in the ghettos of Abidjan, the only way to survive was by giving due respect to "elders", who were not necessarily older, but who had lived there longer and were assumed to know more about life. At the RSCI, there were no thieves, no "*débalousseurs*"[14], but Kassoum quickly realised that, like Le Colosse, the RSCI was a ghetto. Surviving in a ghetto was something he knew how to do. Behind his naïve air, he was two steps ahead of everyone else. He didn't balk when the moron on the second floor, whose job he had covered for a week, refused to pay him a single franc for the fruits of his labour. He discreetly slipped into the role of errand boy for Jean-Marie, godfather of room allocations and pseudo-president of the residents' association for this crumbling ruin. Then, one day, came the opportunity that he had been waiting for. In the ghetto, such opportunities made you an equal, but most of all, it determined the marks of respect to which you would be entitled. That day, in front of an astonished coterie of residents, he "planted a python"; he delivered a

---

14 Author's note: A Nouchi term for a pickpocket or bag snatcher.

magisterial head-butt to an "outsider" who had been har-
assing one of the residents. Something to do with money
he owed. The beef had nothing whatsoever to do with
Kassoum. He simply used a "Colosse kiss" as they called
it in the ghetto, to prove that he could handle himself and
to show the other residents that, now he that was part of
the "family", they could count on him. The message came
through loud and clear. All ghettos in the world are the
same. The following morning, Jean-Marie introduced him
to Uncle Ferdinand and by the following evening Kassoum
was working his first shift as a security guard at the abandoned mills, being dragged around by a huge hound called
Joseph: it was his first job, the first real job he had had in
his life.

"Look closely: remote security, personal bodyguard
detail, armoured cash transport, sensitive sites, advanced
fire-prevention techniques, nuclear power plants, mega-
structures, etc., all the really profitable parts of the security
sector, the ones that are supposedly technically complex,
are handled by White officers. Shoplifting, thefts from
building sites, squatter prevention, tallying entries and
exits, monitoring variations on control screens, providing
a visible deterrence, manning barriers during concerts or
public events, etc., none of these things are particularly
complicated. But in a large company, it means more staff,
more social security payments, more taxes, more logis-
tics – in short, more problems for very little extra money.
It quickly became apparent that sub-contracting was the
way to carry on making money while getting others to

do the work. Pure capitalism. These simple tasks could be entrusted to Black guys. To boot, when there is a great need for manpower, they can easily get their "brothers" involved. It's not even about racism; it's not about the colour of your skin. It's all about folding money. This is how Uncle Ferdinand and all the old Ivorians in Paris set up the companies they inaccurately call security firms. The reason the system works, Kassoum, is because when it comes down to it, there's nothing to monitor. Even today, a minimal Black presence is enough for people to feel that a site is secure. It's the feeling, Kassoum, the feeling: what we provide is the feeling of security.

"But after what's just happened in New York, let me tell you, the Whites will take matters into their own hands. Finally, there are things that need to be monitored, intruders would need to be intercepted, sites that need to be professionally secured. The feeling of insecurity now looms larger than the Twin Towers, even if you stacked them on top of each other. It will take a lot to address that feeling of insecurity. Certainly a lot more than a minimal Black presence. From now on, the job requirements in the security sector will be very high. Any employer will want to go through our paperwork with a fine-tooth comb before they allow us to stand in front of a fucking billboard.

"The whole planet has been plunged into the age of paranoia, Kassoum, an era of law and order. After today, the world will never be the same again. Take my word for it: a month from now, you and I won't have a job. Or at least, not with Uncle Ferdinand."

151

Kassoum remembered. Everything had happened exactly as Ossiri had predicted. Idle hours gradually stretched out until they completely disappeared. After a few months, Uncle Ferdinand's Peugeot 205 stopped coming to the RSCI to pick up workers. Security firms now needed to apply for a special permit from the préfecture de Police to continue to operate. Even routine jobs like security assistant or night watchman, the sort of jobs Kassoum had been doing for years, required a certificate that the préfecture issued only after examining an applicant's residence permit and an ensuring that his criminal record was as unsullied by crime as the Virgin Mary's womb was of Palestinian cock. The people who had once worked for Uncle Ferdinand thought that, any day now, he would get this famous permit and things would go back to how they had been. Those who had never worked with him, and those he had fired for one reason or another, claimed that Ferdinand had filed for bankruptcy long ago but was brazenly lying about getting a permit. Just so he did not have to pay the people the salaries he still owed. And since troubles come not as single spies but surrounded by brothers, sisters and cousins, there were rumours that everyone was about to be evicted from the RSCI. Those who had lived there for a long time said they had heard it all before. They assumed that, as usual, nothing would actually happen, that no-one would have the balls to throw them and their families out into the street in the dead of winter. Those who had arrived more recently did not dare contradict the elders, but they secretly began looking for other places to stay, just in case.

In Paris, the Ponia, the residence of the Revolutionary Society of Students from the Cote d'Ivoire, and a number of legendary buildings squatted by members of the African community had already seen forced evictions despite the routine protests from left-wing associations and professional organisations who spoke up for the homeless and the disadvantaged. Those more recently arrived were more pragmatic, or more resigned, but they were careful not to show it to others.

At the RSCI, every rumour was half-false or half-true. And in an atmosphere of enforced idleness, they proliferated. Now that there were no security jobs, no-one at the RSCI had work. So, rumours were rife. As in every ghetto in the world, the inhabitants of the RSCI rarely moved around. They kept to themselves, holed up in their misery, unable even to take a stroll in the fresh air on the deck of their prison ship. There were no walls, no jailer to physically imprison them. The cafés on the place d'Italie were a two-minute walk away, the trendy bars of the Butte-aux-Cailles only five minutes'. The gardens of Bercy were three métro stops. Even the grounds of Pitié-Salpêtrière Hospital, a stone's throw from the RSCI, offered an oasis in the middle of Paris for anyone prepared to take a stroll. But for most human beings, a ghetto, whether rich or poor, narrows the horizon, it creates prison bars in the mind. It was as though they felt that if they left the RSCI, they might get used to better things, normal things: simple things like a clean lobby, clean toilets, a working flush system, level stairs, pristine walls, an absence of mice and cockroaches, empty rubbish bins... "The worst thing about poverty is becoming accustomed to what you do not have."[15] Kassoum understood ghetto syndrome all too well. He had experienced it in Le Colosse. He was not about to go through it again in Paris. He saw Ossiri leave the RSCI every morning and come home late at night. He decided to follow him.

A visit to the freely accessible areas of the Louvre; an exhibition of photography in a strange house near Saint-Paul, not far from the place de la Bastille; a long walk along the Canal de l'Ourcq; a stroll through Père Lachaise cemetery; several visits to White men and women who were obviously his friends; an evening in the eighteenth arrondissement, a stone's throw from the African Market of Château Rouge, at the house of someone from the Antilles where there were people of every imaginable complexion; a number of small free concerts in bars around Belleville; drinking coffee on café terraces where people talked to each other and no-one seemed to notice that you came from a Treichville ghetto; a visit to a media library that contained more CDs of African music than in all of Abidjan; a nightclub in Bastille where all the bouncers were former gangsters from Abobo;[16] even a play in a tiny little room in Ménilmontant... When he followed Ossiri, Kassoum did things he had never imagined. In four weeks, he saw more

15 Author's note: Michel Alex Kipré, *Sang Pansé*, published by Harmattan-FratMat.
16 Author's note: A working-class neighbourhood in the north of Abidjan.

places, understood more culture, met more people, learned more things than he had in four years living in France, holed up at the RSCI. In four weeks, Kassoum came to realise that he was not simply *abroad*; he had *travelled*. Ossiri showed him that he was living in another culture, another world, one filled with beauty and ugliness, with yawning chasms and Himalayan peaks, like everywhere else. Ossiri made him understand how rich he was simply because he had travelled. "Kassoum, you're a better man simply because you're here. Better than the people in Le Colosse who will never see Paris. Better than the people in Paris who will never see Le Colosse." One afternoon, as they were walking down the boulevard de l'Hôpital towards the Seine, Ossiri told him to look up. At first, Kassoum saw nothing. Look, Ossiri insisted. Kassoum felt a little foolish, standing on the pavement with his head in the air, staring at a blue, cloudless sky. Blue. Cloudless. Blue. The sky was blue. Trivial as it might seem, Kassoum understood what Ossiri had been trying to make him see. In Abidjan, the sky was never blue. It was always filled with whole herds of clouds in varying shades of grey. The wind, their invisible shepherd, brought them here to graze, and here they swelled and thickened, swelled to become a single massive grey-black cumulonimbus, before coming to earth as thunderous tropical rain. This clear, azure sky above the gare d'Austerlitz, this deep blue streaked by the vapour trails of long-haul flights... Kassoum was beginning to discover.

Kassoum was also beginning to get to know Ossiri. The shy and reserved boy who lived at the RSCI was utterly unlike the stellar, generous being who showed him around Paris and made him see life from a perspective different to that of an undocumented immigrant constantly fearful of being stopped by the police. At the RSCI, everyone laughed at Ossiri's slightly precocious quirks. He was constantly washing his hands. He cleaned the toilet and the shower on the landing. He had a personal rubbish bin that he took out and emptied into the public bins on the boulevard. He was always the first to wake up, roll up his sleeping mat, put it in a corner and head out, carrying a bag that contained almost everything he owned. Rumour had it that he was the son of an obsessive White man back in Abidjan, which would explain why he felt compelled to do housework. But the one thing that no-one understood about Ossiri was respect, even the deference shown him by the devious old owl, Jean-Marie. He never ranted at Ossiri to pay his rent, never complained when, from time to time, Ossiri set up his mattress in the old study. The study was Jean-Marie's biggest money-spinner. He rented it out for all kinds of community events. It was particularly popular for funerals, especially among the people for whom funerals were the ultimate social occasions. Whenever a Bété died anywhere on the planet, a vigil was held in every place he had a brother, a sister, a son, a daughter or even a distant cousin. These usually took place on Friday or Saturday, to adapt to the modern working week. During the vigil, donations sometimes amounting to astronomical sums were raised and handed over to a representative of the grieving family. Suffice it to say that in the difficult lives of Bété immigrants living in Paris, the death of a close relative was not necessarily bad news. Most of the Bété families in Paris organised their vigils at the RSCI. It was cheap to rent the study and none of the Ivorians in the old building would complain about the noise from the Bété funeral. For cultural reasons. Besides, most of them were undocumented. For obvious reasons, no-one would dare call the police to complain about a disturbance of the peace. Jean-Marie prospered. The study was the only room in the cesspit of the RSCI that was properly maintained. Jean-Marie guarded it jealously. Which was one of the reasons people were surprised that he did not complain when Ossiri decided to spend time there.

From November 1 to March 31, there was a moratorium on evicting any tenant in Paris, honest or dishonest, or any resident whether legal or illegal, assuming they were permanently domiciled there – i.e. had a mattress and blanket. Ossiri did not know whether this was simply a custom or one of the labyrinthine laws from the intractable Napoleonic civil code that still governed the lives of the French and their colonies throughout the world, including Côte d'Ivoire. He told Kassoum that it was a kind of humanitarian agreement made necessary by meteorology. At this latitude, everyone, even Monsieur Thénardier, Cosette's wicked "uncle" in *Les Misérables*, realised that being forced to sleep outside in winter and risk freezing to death was no joke. The eviction notice for the residents of 150 boulevard Vincent-Auriol came during the month of March. Astronomically, winter ends on March 21. In deeply antagonistic terms, the eviction notice urged all residents to vacate the property before March 31, the bureaucratic end of winter. If they had not complied before this date, then they would be forcibly evicted by the police on April 1, the first day after the winter break. This was serious. When local humanitarian associations arrived to support the RSCI residents, they realised that it was all over. When the Housing Rights Association, the Restaurants du Cœur and Médecins du Monde and sundry humanitarian associations come knocking, you know you are up shit creek. While their members felt they were Christians who brought hope through social responsibility, to undocumented immigrants and the homeless, they were virtue-signalling symbols of their despair and a realistic portrait of their tragic situation. Only a week remained to find alternative accommodation when Kassoum realised that every single resident of the RSCI already had a fallback position. But what mattered during the last days before the eviction was being as active as possible "on the frontlines of the resistance". It was important to show, to demonstrate, as dramatically as possible, how wrong it was to throw poor, helpless Black people out into the streets. Your outrage and your anger had to be shouted from the rooftops, preferably in the pithiest possible slogans. The media lapped up outrage when it was couched in elegant grammatical phrases. This was a media showdown. With Jean-Marie leading the charge, the whole of the RSCI was suddenly transformed into a hotbed of radical leftists, staunch enemies of selfish capitalism, opponents of social injustice. Every resident had become an innocent victim being scarified on the altar of "xenophobic policies" by a "fascist government". The sheer size of the building, the large number of residents and the involvement of neighbourhood associations attracted a number of media outlets.

A battle ensued among the residents of the RSCI for the coveted title of spokesperson for the community. The moment a Shure, Rode, Sony or Sennheiser microphone was proffered, the moment a TV camera flashed its Zeiss lens, there was a battle of the words, a war of spokespersons. Everyone was suddenly seized by *MSB syndrome*.

In the mid-1990s, in an attempt to avoid being deported from France, a group of undocumented immigrants sought sanctuary in the church of Saint-Bernard de la Chapelle in the eighteenth arrondissement. Blessed France, handmaiden of the church, would not dare invade a place where the two-thousand-year-old communion of the Holy Eucharist took place every Sunday. Sometimes, even undocumented immigrants have brilliant ideas. The police laid siege to the church. The media came running to bear witness to this unseemly stand-off. For the duration of the siege, both the left- and the right-wing press found a blue-eyed boy from Senegal who answered to the caricatural name of Mamadou. His actual name was Ababacar Diop, but when dealing with a Negro, you say Mamadou; it's simpler and easier to pronounce. Mamadou was photogenic, and he spoke French without too much of an accent – much better than the illiterates he was holed up with inside the chapel. Finally, the whole of France could put a face and a voice to the concept of an undocumented immigrant, an illegal, an irregular. It goes without saying that neither widespread support, nor the finely honed phrases of Mamadou, could stop riot police brutally and spectacularly storming the church. On the orders of the Minister of the Interior, Jean-Louis Debré, riot police broke down the church doors with axes and battering rams. A positively medieval incursion. Undocumented migrants, priests, nuns, journalists, supportive neighbours, left-wing activists, random passers-by . . . every single person – irrespective of race and ethnicity for once – was forcibly thrown out of the church. After an easy Pantone-sorting process, all the Blacks were bundled into police vans with sirens wailing and blue lights flashing. The engine of the charter planes on the runway at Roissy were already idling, so it was not long before the undocumented immigrants found themselves in Dakar or Bamako. We do not know whether Mamadou went along for the ride. Nor do we really know how, some months later, our beloved Mamadou was granted a visa. His story was finally "fairytale-ised" shortly afterwards when he was awarded millions of francs in a curious story of domain name plagiarism by Vivendi Universal. Ever since, at every highly publicised eviction, everyone has dreamed of being The Mamadou. *MSB syndrome*: *Mamadou of Saint-Bernard syndrome*.

Jean-Marie was clearly the front runner in this battle. But unfortunately for him, the eviction was not widely covered by the media. There must have been more spectacular stories in the national and international news at the time. And besides, not long before, the mass evictions at an African squat in Arcueil had made the story less compelling. In Arcueil, famous White actors and actresses had exposed themselves in defence of The Cause, thereby stealing the limelight from any Black spokespeople. As a result, the riot police were able to evict the residents of the RSCI with minimal fuss or difficulty. There was a little shouting, a little grandstanding, but deep down, no-one could reasonably fight for the right to carry on living in a decrepit and unsanitary building. No-one, reasonably.

Ossiri had already found a small, shared apartment above the Chapelle des Lombards, a nightclub not far from the place de la Bastille. He moved in with Kassoum. In theory, it was the home to the club bouncer. Sort of. Ossiri had known Zandro, the nightclub heavy, back in Abidjan. They had regularly been pitched against each other during school brawls. When Ossiri randomly bumped into Zandro one summer day outside the Bastille Opera, the memory of those stupid brawls of the time brought them together. At night, while Zandro was manning the door of "the Chapel" below, Ossiri and Kassoum were sleeping upstairs, lulled by the subwoofer vibrations. During the day, it was the physiognomist's turn to sleep while Ossiri and Kassoum went looking for a job. Because, thanks to all of Ossiri's acquaintances and friends, Kassoum always found work. Removals, setting up and dismantling market stalls, removing rubble, gardening, etc. – wherever there was work to be found, Kassoum was on hand. But, paradoxically, when terrorist attacks began to immigrate to Europe with the Madrid train bombings, the security sector was once again opened up to people like Kassoum with dubious legal status. The London 7/7 attacks further hastened this seeming illogical impetus. People needed more and more hands and eyes to rummage through bags, through trash cans, to monitor access, to decide on who could enter ... The "Standing Heavies" were back. Though not the sub-contractors run by old Ivorians from France. Their companies had long since gone bankrupt, engulfed as they were by a lack of customer confidence and the new permits. The new employers, those would secure the contracts and could get the necessary permits, were all White.

The buzz of an intercom, the quick glance at the CCTV monitor, press of a button, click of the lock, swish of the double-entrance security door opening, a harried man or woman enters, hello muttered between clenched teeth, handbags and metal objects placed in a plastic tray on a conveyor belt, harried man or woman steps through security gate, plastic tray of handbags and metal objects passes through an X-ray machine, quick glance at X-ray screen, harried man or woman collects their belongings, mutters thanks between clenched teeth, harried man or woman disappears down the lobby towards the lifts: next ... This simple, invariable protocol is his job. In the little office lit by fluorescent bulbs, the picture window with its wood-veneer PVC frame affords a breathtaking view of the security gate, his security gate. The glass is apparently bulletproof; he takes the manufacturers at their word.

In the middle of this picture window, the head and torso of the Black man we can see is Kassoum. He is dressed in a black blazer, white shirt, black tie. In this chilly, spartan atmosphere, he is like one more decorative element of a clean-line, sub-Bauhaus design concept. An interactive element. Because we see him smile broadly at every hello muttered through clenched teeth by the harried men and women passing him. And after each cursory "thank you", when he presses the button to admit them, Kassoum never misses the opportunity to aim a stentorian "Have a nice day!" at the backs of their heads as they race for the lifts. Rarely does the security gate emit its shrill wail or the X-ray machine flag up some curio in the countless bags that pass through it each day. But when it does, Kassoum has only to press a button to notify the Command Post, the famous CP, on the first floor, just above his head. Hierarchical division of labour. Then a security guard appears. As if by magic. The element of surprise is intended to unsettle. The suspicious individual, whether it is the King of Lesotho or the Queen of England in person, is immediately taken into a small search room while the other harried men and women continue to enter as if nothing has happened. Harried men and women have no time to deal with some idiot who forgot to take a keyring out of his pocket before going through the security gate. Though it could just as easily be a terrorist trying to smuggle a Kalashnikov in his underpants. One of those extremists, ideally an Arab

Muslim, who thirsts for the blood of the innocent Westerners working at one of the world's largest biomedical companies. To harried men and women, there is no difference between the thickhead and the terrorist. They do not have the time to think about the people who set off alarms. It is precisely to avoid this that the company pays for a phalanx of security guards and a battery of expensive security equipment.

Kassoum is on the job; the harried men and women can calmly continue being harried every morning. Kassoum only oversees the "entrants". Everyone entering the building is obliged to go pass through there and conform to this ritual. Kassoum's busiest period is the morning. For the rest of the day he takes a few calls on a state-of-the-art telephone with countless buttons, of which he has mastered only three functions: to pick up, hang up and transfer. Before the "entry point", there are the "badgers", the desk that checks ID cards and registers all visitors. It is they who distribute visitors' badges, hence Kassoum's nickname for them. On the far side of the vast lobby is the "leavers" station. There are countless positions and endless complicated procedures. Division of labour. The more sensitive the site, the greater the number of workstations, the more complex the procedures. There is no room here for personal initiative or zeal. Before anything can be done, there is the inevitable torrent of instructions, orders and contractors. At sensitive sites, the job of the security guard is cushy. But for the surfeit of bosses lying in wait in corridors and offices, it would be a good fit for Kassoum. It hardly matters;

this is the most peaceful job he has had since his heyday at Les Grands Moulins de Paris.

He is woken from his reverie by the shrill caterwaul of the metal detector. It's a woman. A very harried woman who looks devastated simply at the prospect of having to step into the search suite. When she shoots him a look of surprise, there is a plea in her green eyes. Green like his wife's eyes. The woman is pregnant, like his wife. His beautiful wife Amélie who will give him a son in less than two weeks. They already know what they will call the child. Kassoum does not press the Command Post alarm button. He waves the harried woman through. Perhaps this could be an instance of gross misconduct. Perhaps the woman is a dangerous terrorist with a fake belly filled with C4-plastic, the preferred explosive of Western terrorists. Perhaps. But on his last day as a security guard, Kassoum is not about to be overly zealous. After seven years living in France, he has finally been granted an appointment at the préfecture de Police. Perhaps tomorrow, he will finally be issued with his first residence permit. Perhaps.

EPILOGUE

Ossiri made Kassoum promise that, from the day he got his residence permit, he would stop doing "paid standing". "I have never seen you as happy as the time we spent together working as gardeners," he said simply. Two days later, Ossiri went out and never came back. No-one phones the police to report an undocumented immigrant as a missing person. Aside from a few questions from close friends, no-one made any effort to find him. Ossiri was no-one to anyone, and to everyone he was no-one. There were rumours that he had gone back to Abidjan. The cousin of a former resident of the RSCI insisted he had seen Ossiri in a shanty town in Adjouffou, a ghetto near the runways of Félix Houphouët-Boigny airport in Abidjan. Ossiri in Adjouffou? Kassoum did not believe it. Besides, how could he have gone back to Abidjan? Deported? Ossiri never took the métro without a valid ticket. True, Ossiri had often talked to him about his recurring dream of the "escort to the border", the bucolic idyll, the massed choir. But Ossiri had a crazy story for every department in every branch of Sephora in France. And besides, everyone knew that before the "escort to the border", you had to go to jail, go directly to jail. The sentence was doubled for undocumented immigrants. A heroin-addicted rapist, a high-profile white-collar criminal or a recidivist crack dealer had a better chance in the courts than a diligent worker without a residence permit. *Dura lex* . . . Ossiri knew that. No, he could not be back in Adjouffou. Kassoum refused to believe it. He simply just felt that he did not need to worry. Street smarts. Misfortune is always much louder than good fortune. One day, as he was changing his jacket, Kassoum found a scribbled note in Ossiri's sloping hand: "Leave the vultures' work to the vultures." Born in Treichville, raised in Abobo-behind-the-railway, seasoned in Le Colosse, travelled most of the way from Abidjan to France to squat at the RSCI, only when he saw these words did Kassoum weep for the first time.

GAUZ' is an author, journalist and screenwriter who grew up in Côte d'Ivoire. After studying biochemistry, he moved to Paris as an undocumented student, working as a security guard before returning to Côte d'Ivoire. His first novel, *Standing Heavy*, came out in 2014 and won the Prix des libraires Gibert Joseph. It was followed by *Comrade Papa*, which won the 2019 Prix Éthiophile and the 2018 Grand prix littéraire d'Afrique noire, and *Black Manoo*. GauZ' is the editor-in-chief of the satirical economic newspaper *News & co* and has written screenplays and documentary films.

FRANK WYNNE is an award-winning writer and translator. His previous translations include works by Virginie Despentes, Javier Cercas and Michel Houellebecq. His translation of *Vernon Subutex I* was shortlisted for the Man Booker International Prize.